JUSTICE BURNING

HELLFIRE BOOK #2

ELLE JAMES

TWISTED PAGE INC

JUSTICE BURNING

HELLFIRE SERIES BOOK #2

ELLE JAMES

New York Times & USA Today

Bestselling Author

EBOOK ISBN: 978-1-62695-053-5

PRINT ISBN: 978-1-62695-054-2

This book is dedicated to the all the men and women who separate from active duty and struggle to find meaning in the civilian world. Thank you for your service. We love you for all you did and do, and the sacrifices you made.

Escape with...

Elle James

aka Myla Jackson

AUTHOR NOTE

Enjoy other great books by Elle James
Hellfire Series
Hellfire, Texas (#1)
Justice Burning (#2)
Smoldering Desire (#3)
Hellfire in High Heels (#4)
Playing With Fire (#5)
Up in Flames (#6) TBD
Total Meltdown (#7) TBD

Visit ellejames.com for more titles and release dates
For hot cowboys, visit her alter ego Myla Jackson at
mylajackson.com and join Elle James and Myla
Jackson's Newsletter at
http://ellejames.com/ElleContact.htm

CHAPTER 1

"THE BASTARD!" Phoebe Sinclair's usual easy-going demeanor had taken a major hit. She checked the rearview mirror, couldn't see anything past the train of her wedding dress flying out behind her. When she'd discovered her fiancé had skipped out on the wedding just seconds before she was due to walk down the aisle, she'd practically jumped into the convertible. He'd left the church, no explanation, no excuses. Which meant Phoebe would have had to face her parents and their guests to break the news alone. There wouldn't be a wedding. The groom had run out on her.

Jilted.

Never mind she'd already been having extremely cold feet. Two hours earlier, she'd been a nervous bride, convinced she was making a huge mistake by marrying a man her father had selected as perfect husband material for his darling daughter. Her mother had argued that Ryan would help elevate her social status even more. Not that Phoebe cared two hoots about status.

Phoebe, the dutiful daughter who'd always done what her parents wanted, who never had anxiety issues, could have used one of her mother's anti-anxiety pills. On the very verge of walking down the aisle of the church to promise to love, honor and cherish Ryan Bratton, a colleague of her father's, she'd asked herself *why?* Why was she marrying a man with whom she didn't have much in common? Why was she allowing her parents to choose her husband? Why had she let herself be swept into the whole wedding experience?

The pathetic answer was that all of her Dallas debutante friends were either engaged or married. Some were pregnant with their first babies.

Tick tock, tick tock.

Her damned biological clock had been ticking pretty darned loud when her father proclaimed it was time to get married and produce heirs. He wasn't getting any younger and he wanted to know he'd have someone to pass the oil speculation business to when he was gone.

Phoebe slowed behind a tractor hauling a large round hay bale. Wisps of straw flew over the top of the convertible's windshield, tangling in her hair. Swerving toward the center of the road, she peered around the big green John Deere. The lane was clear and she sped past.

Her father could sell the damned business for all she cared. Phoebe had never had a head for business, preferring to hang out with the horses on their ranch. She hadn't really been that interested in dating, finding most of the men in her parents' circle either old like her father, greedy or lazy. When she went out on dates, many of the men were more interested in her father's assets than in her own.

She'd stared into the full-length mirror, her heart pounding, perspiration popping out on her forehead and upper lip, after her mother had applied makeup to her face. Phoebe couldn't do it. She didn't love Ryan. Though her father thought highly of him, his opinion of Ryan wasn't enough.

Sure, he'd had her grandmother's locket professionally reworked by a jeweler, with a brand new chain and a picture of her grandmother inside. The extremely thoughtful gift had almost convinced her he was the man she needed. But standing in front of the mirror, staring at the stranger in the white dress, about to marry a man she really didn't know, she'd started into a full-on panic attack.

Her mother had entered the room, slapped a paper bag into her hand and told her to breathe into the bag. Then her mother had straightened her veil, patted powder on her face and turned her toward the door with a parting comment, "Don't embarrass me."

Her mother moved inside the sanctuary to take her seat.

Phoebe stood outside the door, waiting for the cue for her bridesmaids to make the long trip down the aisle ahead of her. Something had held up the ceremony. Five minutes turned to ten but her cue didn't come.

One of the groomsmen ducked out of the sanctuary, spotted her and waved her back toward the anterooms.

Phoebe handed her bouquet to her maid of honor, a silly society girl her mother had chosen since Phoebe didn't have many girlfriends suitable to wear the ridiculous bridesmaid gowns. "I'll be a moment." Phoebe hurriedly joined the groomsman.

He glanced over her shoulder at the others watching and then leaned close to whisper, "We have a problem."

Her heart had fluttered, her stomach roiling. "What's wrong?"

The man tugged at his collar as if the tie constricted his vocal cords.

Phoebe wanted to take a hold of the tie and tug on it herself. Hard. "Spit it out," she finally said.

He took a deep breath and blurted, "Ryan disappeared."

"What?" And her mother had been afraid *Phoebe* would embarrass her. "He ran out? Did he say anything before he disappeared?"

The young man's face turned a bright red and he shook his head.

"You have got to be kidding." Surely Ryan had only gone to the restroom or outside to catch a breath of fresh air. Phoebe stormed off toward the room the groom was supposed to use for wedding preparations. Flinging open the door, she marched in. "Ryan, you better get your scrawny ass up to the altar…"

The room was empty. Ryan and his tuxedo were gone.

"Really?" she cried. "*You* got cold feet?" Blood pounded in her ears. She stared around the room, hoping he was hiding somewhere and going to spring out and say *surprise!*

With a sanctuary full of five hundred of her parents' closest friends waiting for the wedding to start, Phoebe didn't know what to do. She'd agreed to marry Ryan, not because she particularly loved him, but because no one else had come along in her thirty-one years who inspired the soul-defining passion she had expected to come with falling in love. Ryan could kiss okay and he'd tried to please her when they'd been more intimate. Still…nothing. No sparks, no earth-shaking anything. Surely all those romance novels she'd read late into the night weren't all pure fantasy.

Phoebe had begun to think she didn't have the romantic gene in her body, so she'd settled for Ryan.

Now, he'd skipped out. Jilted her at the altar and left her with the task of telling all the five hundred strangers her fiancé hadn't wanted to marry her after all. "I could kill him," she said.

"Excuse me?" a voice said behind her.

With a little scream, she spun to face Ryan's best man, Warren Ledbetter. "Did you know he was thinking of backing out of this circus of a wedding?" she demanded.

He shook his head. "He told me to go on to the sanctuary, that he'd be there momentarily. That was fifteen minutes ago."

"Well, I'm not telling all those people this event isn't happening." She waved a hand toward the church. "I'm not taking the rap for it. My father and mother will be livid after spending a small fortune on this show."

Warren's eyes widened. "What are you going to do?"

"I don't know." She glanced around the room and over her shoulder at the hallway. The choice had come down to either face her parents and the sanctuary full of people, or leave and hoping her parents didn't hate her for eternity.

Phoebe's feet, in the white satin pumps, took her toward the door. When the dutiful daughter should have turned left to go to the sanctuary, she turned right. Rather than face her parents, Phoebe opted to run. Yes, leaving was the coward's way out, but she'd had enough of her parents running her life, choosing her clothes, her friends and her husband.

She'd run out the side door of the church nursery to a playground where she hurried past the swings and play fort. Out in the Texas sunshine, she lifted her skirts and ran, breathing in the fresh taste of freedom. If Ryan could skip out of a wedding neither of them really wanted, so could she.

Phoebe dared to dream of a life she chose to live. She could get a job, pay her own way, make her own friends and really live. The faster she ran, the better she felt until she kicked off her heels and sprinted toward the parking lot out front.

Before she reached it, Phoebe ground to a stop. She'd arrived in her parents' chauffeur-driven town car. The church was off the usual routes of taxi drivers, and she didn't have any money to pay a driver. Nor did she have a cell phone to call for a pick up. Her newfound freedom took a turn for the worst.

Then she spied the wedding car, a sleek black Cadillac convertible with specially decorated cans tied with silk ribbons beneath the bumper, parked outside the door to the church's banquet hall where the reception was to be held after the wedding. A banner affixed to the trunk read JUST MARRIED. Daring to hope, she inched up to the driver's side of the vehicle and looked inside.

Hope flared in her chest at the sight of the keys in the ignition.

Gathering her skirts, she jumped in, twisted the key and drove away from the church, leaving behind what would be her disappointed, embarrassed parents and a life she never seemed to fit into.

Thus started the great adventure.

Phoebe wore a wedding dress, didn't have a penny tucked away on any part of her body, and had taken her fiancé's convertible. Not until she'd left Dallas and put over a hundred miles between her and the wedding guests did the adrenaline wear off. She could be charged with grand theft auto. The car belonged to her delinquent fiancé, not her. At the moment that thought struck, she swerved to the side of the road and bumped over some trash on the shoulder. Her heart raced, and she tried to think. She could ditch the car and call the police to tell them where they could find it. Or she could just ditch the car in some backwater town and…and…what?

She couldn't steal another. Without a dollar on her, she couldn't buy a bus ticket or a rent a car. Damn. She should have thought this escape through a little more thoroughly. One thing was certain, she couldn't stay on the side of the road. A sign a few miles back indicated a town was coming up. What was the name? Hellfire? A peculiar name for a town.

Her stomach rumbled, reminding her she hadn't eaten since the night before. Maybe she could stop there, find a job and work for food. With a little bit of a plan in mind, she drove toward the town. She hadn't gone more than a quarter of a mile when a sharp pop sounded, and the car pulled to the right.

Phoebe steered off the road and got out. Wadding up her skirt, she folded it over her arm and padded around the front of the car, gravel and grass digging into her tender bare feet. As she'd suspected, the right front tire was flat. Great. Her shoulders slumped. She'd never changed a flat tire in her life and her father had never demonstrated the process. He'd whip out his cell phone, call for roadside assistance and wait until help arrived. Phoebe didn't have that luxury, with neither a cell phone, nor a roadside assistance service that didn't belong to her daddy. Not to mention, that wasn't what independent women did. How the hell did one change a flat tire?

She walked back around to the driver's side and pulled the keys from the ignition. When she'd seen movies where the characters had to change a tire, they always went to the trunk. The spare tire should be in the trunk. It stood to reason, the tools to change the flat would be in the trunk as well. Keys in hand, she walked to the back of the vehicle, and hit the button to pop open the trunk.

With her dress in hand, barefooted, broke and determined, she leaned over and studied the space. A blanket lay across a rather large lump in the back. Hopefully the spare tire. Phoebe grabbed the blanket and yanked it off.

She gasped and staggered backward, all the blood

draining from her head. This couldn't be happening. *No. No. No.* Phoebe pressed her hand to her lips and edged closer to look again, praying she'd imagined what she'd seen.

Nope.

The lump beneath the blanket was none other than her missing groom, Ryan. Based on his waxy gray face and open eyes staring at nothing, the man was well and truly dead.

Sweet Jesus. Oh, sweet Jesus. Phoebe bit down on her bottom lip. Had she checked the trunk before she'd gone one hundred miles, would he have been alive enough to resuscitate? She gulped. Had she killed him by not checking? Though she hadn't really loved him, she never wished him dead.

The next thought hit her square in the gut. She'd stolen Ryan's car, run out on the wedding, and now had his dead body in the back of the vehicle. To make it worse, she had a witness who could state he heard her say, *I'll kill him.* The best man had been there when she'd gone to find Ryan.

When the cops caught up with her and Ryan's car, they'd find his body, receive testimony from his best man and presume Phoebe had killed him. Her independence would come to a screeching halt when she was arrested, booked and thrown in jail for the rest of her life.

Her head spinning, Phoebe stood back, looking around at the rolling grasslands. Not a car was in sight. She couldn't just walk away. Barefoot, no telling how far to the nearest town, she wouldn't make it. Phoebe hadn't planned to start a new life on the lam for a murder she didn't commit.

Scrambling for something, *anything*, she could do to get out of the mess she'd landed in, she slammed the trunk, hurried around the car and jumped into the driver's seat. The wind chose that moment to pick up and her dress billowed around her as she pulled forward on the flat tire, bumping along the shoulder of the road. Her skirt flew up in her face. Trying to flatten it so that she could see, she shifted her foot to hit the brake, but she hit the accelerator instead. The convertible leaped forward, ran off the road and slammed into a fence post, throwing Phoebe forward, banging her forehead against the steering wheel. She saw stars that quickly changed to bright blue strobes. As her vision cleared, she realized the lights were attached to a police vehicle.

Could her day get any worse?

"UNIT 470, we have a report of some teenagers drag racing on farm to market road 476 at the old Dunwitty grain silo."

"10-4." Deputy Nash Grayson slowed the sheriff's deputy SUV, checked the road ahead leading into Hellfire, and glanced in his rearview mirror. No one coming. No one going. Quiet, placid, small-town

Texas, where nothing much happened. He made a U-turn and headed back out into the countryside.

Thirteen months ago, he'd been in full combat gear, slipping through the streets of a small village in Afghanistan, searching for Taliban rebels. His fourth tour to the Middle East, he knew the drill. Kill the bad guys, not the civilians.

The nation he was sworn to defend didn't understand how difficult it was to tell the difference. A smiling Afghan approaching a checkpoint might have explosives strapped to his waist beneath the robe he wore. Or a mother might send her child armed with a grenade into a group of soldiers visiting an orphanage. Over there, he had to remain vigilant. Hell, he'd needed eyes in the back of his head. Always alert, always listening and looking for sudden movement.

After a year back in his hometown of Hellfire, he still jumped at loud noises and dropped into a fighting stance when someone sneaked up behind him. But the bucolic life of the small town had helped him learn to breathe deeply again. Well, not too deeply when the wind blew from the direction of the local stockyard. The stench of cattle crap and urine filled the air on those days.

Other than the usual teenaged hijinks and an occasional domestic quarrel, things were pretty laid back. Almost too much so. Thankfully, when he wasn't on the job, Nash had the family ranch to retreat to. There, he could work with the animals and burn off some of his restless energy.

Although he was nearing the end of his shift, Nash didn't mind checking out the drag racing report. A typical Saturday in the country. Hellfire didn't have a bowling alley or movie theater. The only organized activities available to the kids were football and rodeo. High school football games drew everyone out on Friday evenings in the fall. Which left Saturday and Sunday to do chores before the kids returned to school and parents to work on Monday. But after chores, the teens liked to gather at the town's only fast food drive-in or find a place to raise hell out in the countryside. Everything from cow-tipping to mud-riding in the bottoms.

Today's hell-raising just happened to be drag racing.

Nash pulled into the rutted gravel road leading to the abandoned Dunwitty silos. Apparently the race was in full swing, because all eyes were on the vehicles at the center of the mob. Two tricked-out trucks, with knobby tires and fat chrome exhaust pipes, shot out of the crowd of young people and barreled along the wide gravel road running half a mile in length. Their engines rumbled, the sound reverberating through the warm, late-afternoon air.

Guys in jeans, cowboy boots and hats punched the air, whooping and hollering. Girls in frayed cutoffs and shirts tied at their midriffs, laughed and screamed for the drivers to go faster.

Nothing Nash could do at that point would slow the racing trucks. If he didn't know they were trespassing, he'd enjoy the race and then slip away before anyone was the wiser about his presence there.

But this was Dunwitty's place and the clearly posted NO TRESPASSING signs out front were all the rules Nash needed. He followed the rules, the structure of his job and his life giving him comfort.

When the trucks reached the end of the road, the crowd of young people shouted, yelled, hooted and whistled for the winner. The trucks turned around and drove back to the silos, stopping as the kids converged on them.

Nash got out of his vehicle. Time to spoil the fun.

One young man, Johnny Austin, spotted Nash before he reached the edge of the crowd. "Time to leave," he shouted, loud enough to be heard over the noise of the celebration.

All faces turned toward him.

With a wave, Nash jerked his head toward the silos. "Sorry, folks. I gotta break it up. You're trespassing."

"Aw," the group said as a collective.

The guys and girls piled into the cars and trucks and filed out of the silo area, one by one.

Once they'd all gone, Nash climbed into his SUV and headed back to town to hang up his hat and go home. Another day, another dollar. The excitement was killing him. He chuckled. He'd thought about going to work in Houston, where a shooting occurred every day. Maybe more. But he liked being near the ranch, the horses and cattle. He'd missed it when he'd been on active duty.

Perhaps he needed a woman in his life. Like his brother Becket, who'd never been happier. Up until Kinsey had come back into his brother's life, Nash had been content to be a bachelor. Seeing them together, always touching and kissing...Never mind the headboard banging and springs squeaking into the wee hours of the morning. Nash had gone so far as to sleep in the barn a few times, or asked for the night shift to avoid the happy copulating going on in the ranch house master bedroom.

Yeah, Houston was looking more and more like a possibility.

Ahead, he spied a strange sight. A shiny black convertible, with cans strung out behind and a banner proclaiming JUST MARRIED, sped toward town, weaving side to side, white fabric ballooning up from the driver's seat like a parachute.

His interest spiked, and he increased his speed, hoping to catch up to the car to check it out.

CHAPTER 2

No. No. No.

This could not be happening. Phoebe tried to back away from the fence post, but the convertible's rear tires spun in the dry Texas dust. The front bumper, seeming to have adhered to the fence post, refused to let go.

To make her shithole of a life worse, a county sheriff's SUV pulled to a stop on the pavement. A man in a dark brown uniform, wearing a black cowboy hat with a badge pinned to it stepped out. He hurried down into the ditch, arriving at her door all too soon. "Ma'am, are you okay?"

The wind picked up again and lifted the dress, smothering her face. Phoebe struggled to keep it down, failing miserably. In a stolen car, with a dead body in the trunk, she was going to jail. No doubt in her mind. If by some slim chance, she could get away, maybe she could hide the body, or take it back to the church where all of this had begun. Yeah, she could take back the car and the body.

"Excuse me, ma'am."

"Huh?" She blinked and stared into the startling blue eyes of the sheriff's deputy looking down at her.

He tipped his hat. "I'm Deputy Grayson. I asked if you were okay." He gave a hint of a smile, making a ruggedly handsome face even more attractive.

At least if she was to be arrested, she'd be frisked by a cute deputy. She giggled, hysteria threatening to take over.

"Do you need help?" he asked.

Did she need help? Lord knew she needed help, but this deputy wasn't the kind of help she needed at the moment. Only a miracle could save her from this disaster. "No. I just need help getting the car off the fence."

The deputy rounded the front of the vehicle and shook his head. "Put it in reverse. I'll see if I can kick the bumper loose from the fence post. On three…"

Phoebe nodded, shifted the car into reverse, and waited for his cue.

"One." Bracing a hand on the fence post, he stepped up on the bumper of the car. "Two…three." Grayson bounced hard on the bumper at the same time as Phoebe goosed the gas pedal.

The car broke free of the fence post, the back tires found traction, lumbered up the embankment and back onto the highway, where metal scraped against pavement. For a moment, Phoebe wondered, if she shifted into drive, could the convertible outrun the deputy's vehicle. Then she remembered the flat tire.

Deputy Grayson jogged up the incline and stopped in front of her hood, inspecting the front of her vehicle, his lips twisting. "The bumper's got a nasty dent, and your tire is destroyed. You'll need to change it before you go any farther."

"No. I can't," she said, her heart thumping hard in her chest. She crossed her fingers beneath the folds of her wedding dress. "I don't have a spare."

"Are you sure?" He rolled his hand. "Pop the trunk. Sometimes they're hidden beneath the trunk lining."

"No, really. I checked a few minutes ago." She shifted into drive and glanced over her shoulder. *I have to get away from him.* "I'll just have to drive it flat into the next town."

"No need." He keyed the mic on the radio clipped to his shoulder. "Gretchen, I have a disabled vehicle on the highway east of town. We'll need a tow truck to retrieve it."

"No, no. I can take care of it myself. No need to bother anyone," Phoebe said, her grip tightening on the wheel. "Really."

"No bother. If you'll just hand me the keys, I'll have the service man tow it to the shop, change out the tire, and you can be on your way, barring any damage from the collision with the fence post." Bracing his feet apart, he held out his hand. "First, I'll need to see your license and registration."

"Well...you see..." Heat rose up her cheeks. "I kind of left in a hurry..." She glanced down at her dress. "I forgot to bring my purse with my driver's license." Phoebe glanced up at the deputy.

"Well, I'm sorry, ma'am, but I can't let you drive without a license." He leaned into the window and pointed at the glove box. "Let me see the vehicle registration, please."

Phoebe leaned over the console and fished in the glove box for anything resembling a registration, sweat popping out on her forehead. She found a slim, black folder beneath the convertible's owner's manual. Inside it was...surprise! The registration papers. The vehicle wasn't Ryan's. He'd rented it.

She didn't know whether to be relieved or not. Pulling the paper from the envelope, she handed it to Deputy Grayson. "Is this what you were looking for?"

"Yes, ma'am. Please step out of the vehicle."

"Am I being arrested?" she asked, her pulse hammering through her veins. If he arrested her, would he have the right to search the vehicle? So much for independence. Phoebe could see that she would have to call her father and get him and his expensive attorneys to bail her out of jail.

"No, I hadn't planned on arresting you." He tilted his head. "Should I?"

Phoebe widened her eyes. "N-no. Of course not. I haven't broken any laws." She crossed her fingers behind her back. Except one. Grand theft auto. Although, it was a rental and the man who'd rented it was in it, so she really hadn't stolen it. Had she?

"I can't remember if driving under the influence of a wedding dress was covered in the police academy." Deputy Grayson's lips twitched. "But driving without a license *is* against the law. I won't arrest you if you step out of the vehicle and allow me to escort you to town. When you obtain that license, you can drive."

"Oh. Well. I guess I could send for it. But I can't have you tow the vehicle and change the tire. You see, because I don't have my purse, I don't have money or credit cards to pay for the work." With the registration papers in hand, she pulled the keys from the ignition, gathered her skirts and stepped out of the convertible. "Couldn't we just leave it here for now?"

"Sorry, but we can't leave it on the road." He held out his hand for the registration papers. "Well, this helps. Since this is a rental car, the agency should foot the bill for the towing and the new tire. All it will take is to call them and get them moving on it."

"How nice." Phoebe stared at the trunk, wondering what the rental car company would think about the excess luggage they'd find when they came to collect the vehicle.

No, the body couldn't be there when the rental

car company arrived. Phoebe had to get Ryan out of the trunk before anyone found him. "If the rental car company will take care of the repairs, shouldn't we leave it here for them to collect it? Maybe they have their own wrecker service they like to call," she suggested.

"There's only one in Hellfire. Since you've also bent the front bumper, you might have damaged the radiator or something else in the engine. The car really needs to be checked before you get back on the road."

The man clearly wouldn't let the damned car sit on the side of the road.

While she stood there arguing, another vehicle appeared on the highway, heading in their direction. Phoebe dragged in a deep breath and blew it out.

A wrecker drove past them, turned around, passed them again and then backed up to the convertible. Painted on the side of the truck was the name Grayson's Auto Shop.

Phoebe fought to keep from rolling her eyes. She raised her brows and stared at Deputy Grayson. "A relative of yours?"

The deputy smiled, causing the butterflies in Phoebe's belly to flap. "My brother." Grayson nodded toward the driver of the vehicle. "If you'll ride with me, then my brother will take care of your vehicle."

"Thanks, but I'll ride with the tow truck," she said.

"Are you always so argumentative?" Deputy Grayson asked.

"Not usually." She'd never argued with her folks. Today had been her big day to break all the rules she'd grown up with. And what had it bought her? Potential jail time!

NASH PUT the woman's nerves down to having wrecked and—by the looks of her—being late for a wedding.

Hers.

He found himself thinking it was too bad. She was pretty with long dark red hair tumbling around silky, smooth shoulders. A guy would be lucky to get a pretty thing like her for a wife.

"Is there someone I need to call?" he asked, holding out a hand to help her out of the vehicle. "I take it you might be late for a wedding."

"No." She glanced down at her dress and then up at him, her eyes wide, her bottom lip trembling. "I'm not late for a wedding. I...I changed my mind."

A strange feeling of relief washed over Nash as she placed her hand in his and turned, edging bare feet out of the car door.

"Ma'am, do you have shoes somewhere beneath all of that dress?"

She shook her head and grimaced. "No. I kicked off my shoes as I ran out of the church."

"Do you have a spare pair stowed in the trunk?"

Her eyes widened even more. "No!" She dipped down her head and continued in a more sedate tone. "I brought nothing with me. No purse, no suitcase. The trunk is empty. Really."

"Then let me help you to my vehicle." He leaned down and scooped her out of the car, lifting her into his arms, the dress billowing up around them both.

She squealed and looped an arm around his shoulders. "You don't have to carry me. I can walk barefooted."

"I can see that." He tipped his head toward her scratched feet with the pretty, pale pink nail polish.

"Hey, Nash, whatcha got there?" Rider's chuckle sounded from next to the wrecker.

Nash straightened with his load and faced his brother.

Rider, the closest in age to him of the Grayson brothers, sauntered toward them, a grin spreading across his face.

"Miss—" Damn, he hadn't even gotten her name. "Ma'am, what's your name?"

"Phoebe." She chewed on her lip and then added, "Smith. Phoebe Smith."

Something about her answer didn't sit right, but Nash was more concerned about his brother's dumbass grin. "Miss Smith's had a minor fender bender in a rental vehicle. You'll need to tow it to town, and contact the rental car company to see what they want to do about the crunched bumper and the flat tire."

"Got it." Rider tipped his cowboy hat and held out a hand to Phoebe. "Rider Grayson. Pleased to meet you."

She took his hand and gave him a hesitant smile. "Pleasure's mine." She shot a glance at the car on the side of the road. "If you'd just tow it to town, I'll call the rental car company and make arrangements for it from there."

He touched the brim of his hat. "Yes, ma'am."

"And I've already checked in the trunk," she added. "There isn't a spare. So no need to change the tire."

"I'll tow it, and let it sit until you give me further instructions. Uh, do you always dress this way for outings?" His gaze swept over the dress, and he winked.

Her cheeks flushed and her arm tightened around Grayson's neck. "No. Never."

Ready to move on, Nash frowned at his brother. "If you're done with the questions, I'll escort Phoebe to town. We'll see you there."

Again, Rider touched the brim of his hat. "See you soon."

Damn, Rider had that come-to-hell-with-me smile the ladies loved. By the way Phoebe blushed, she was no different. Didn't Rider get it? The woman had skipped out on a wedding, leaving some poor schmuck standing at the altar, bride-less. She didn't deserve sympathy.

Nash marched to his vehicle, juggled the woman in his arms to half-free a hand from the voluminous folds of the wedding dress and opened the back door. When he leaned down to place her on the seat, her arms locked around his neck and her cheek pressed against his.

"Deputy Grayson," she whispered against his ear.

Her breath warmed Nash's neck, and the scent of honeysuckle wrapped around his senses, making him pause to drag in a deep breath. "Ma'am."

"Do I have to ride in the back?" she asked, her voice shaking. "Please, I don't want to go to jail."

He chuckled and straightened, leaning his head back to look into the most startlingly soft green eyes he'd ever seen. At that moment, they were the color of the moss that grew on the sides of the live oak trees. "It's just to get you to town. Regulations state I can't let anyone but another deputy, or the sheriff, ride up front." He tipped his head toward the front passenger seat, filled with the usual mobile computer and electronics typical of modern police work. "Besides, there isn't much room for you and your dress up front." His lips pulled upward in a smile.

Phoebe chewed on her bottom lip for a moment and then nodded. "I guess it's okay. I just...I never... rode in the back of a police car."

"It's no different than riding in the back seat of

any other vehicle, except the child safety locks are engaged. I'll have to let you out."

She heaved a sigh, the rounded swells of her breasts rising and falling beneath Nash's chin.

Damn, she smelled good, and he bet there was a gorgeous body to match the breasts, all hidden beneath the ridiculous amount of white fluffy material.

Nash deposited her on the back seat, almost dumping her like a bag of hot potatoes before he got too used to holding her against his body. He didn't need complications in his life. Phoebe had complication written all over that pure white wedding dress.

Intent on taking her to town and dropping her off on the nearest sidewalk, he bundled all of the dress inside with her and slammed the back door. Hurrying around the side of the SUV, he glanced across at his brother, standing there with his arms crossed over his chest, that damned grin spreading across his face.

"What?" he demanded, his voice terse, his temper rising.

"Nothing. I just never pictured you carrying a bride." Rider nodded. "Looks good on you, bro."

"Shut up," Nash bit out. "I'm just doing my job."

Rider's grin widened. "Uh-huh. She's pretty, and apparently unattached."

"And passing through." Nash opened the driver's side door, praying the woman in the back seat hadn't heard his brother's words. He didn't want her to get the idea he was at all interested. She'd be gone as soon as she placed a call to whomever she had waiting back at the church.

Nash pulled out onto the road, radioed in to dispatch that he had a passenger and would be dropping her off at the garage. When he'd finished reporting in, he glanced at the woman in the back seat. Her face was pale, her pretty auburn hair a wind-blown mess and she kept chewing on her bottom lip. He found himself wanting to kiss the lip and make her stop worrying it.

Dragging his gaze back to the road ahead, he swerved to miss an escaped Brangus bull, wandering across the road. "Damn." Again, he radioed to dispatch. "Call Raymond Rausch and tell him Francis is loose again. Remind him that he needs to fix the fence on the highway to keep that bull from crossing the road."

"Roger." Gretchen, the dispatcher, responded. "Someday someone will hit that damned bull."

"I sure hope not. I doubt it would hurt the bull, but slamming into him would most likely kill the driver."

"Exactly." Gretchen asked for a mile marker sign and promised to call Rausch immediately.

As he entered town, Nash tried to push aside any feelings of guilt or empathy for the bride in the back seat. The best he could do was to find a telephone for her to make a call to her family back wherever she was from. They could come collect their runaway, and she would be on her way. "My brother has a phone at his shop. I can let you in to use it." He glanced at her in the rearview mirror.

She lifted her chin. "Thank you, but I don't want to call anyone."

"Don't you have family who can come get you?"

Frowning, she shook her head. "I'm not going back."

Great. Now what was he supposed to do with her? "How about a friend?"

"I don't have any friends," she said, her voice firm, but the bottom lip she'd been chewing on trembled.

"Well, I can't just leave you on the street."

She glanced down at the ring on her finger and slipped it off. "Is there anywhere I can sell this ring? I'm sure it's worth something."

He pulled up in front of Rider's garage and shifted into Park. "There is a pawn shop two blocks down. Joe might give you something for it." Staring again at her in the rearview mirror, he added, "Are you sure you want to sell it? Is there no chance of reconciliation between you and your fiancé?"

Her face went another shade paler. "No chance at all."

"I'm sorry to hear that."

"Could you take me to the pawn shop?" She leaned forward, placing her hand on the back of the seat. "If I could sell the ring, I might be able to pay for a new tire."

Already, this Good-Samaritan act was delaying him from getting off duty. But he couldn't drop a barefoot bride on the street. He glanced over his shoulder. "Just so you know, I'm not a taxi service. But after the pawn shop, we're going to the shoe shop with some of that money."

She smiled, for the first time since he'd spotted her on the highway. "Thank you. I'm sorry to be so much trouble." The smile slipped away and her gaze darted out the window.

At the pawn shop, Nash opened the back door for Phoebe. When he bent to lift her out, she placed a hand on his chest. A waft of honeysuckle filled his senses, scrambling his brain cells.

"I can walk. Going barefoot won't kill me," she pointed out.

A moment passed while heat radiated from her palm over his chest and throughout his body. Then he straightened, heat climbing up from the collar of his shirt. He held out a hand, instead. She placed hers in his and allowed him to pull her to her little bare feet with the pink toenail polish. When she stood beside him, the top of her head barely reached his shoulder.

Phoebe bent to gather her train, looped it over her arm and marched into the pawn shop, the sound of the material swishing as she moved louder than any sound her bare feet might have made on the concrete sidewalk.

Why he was thinking about the sound of her bare feet on concrete, Nash didn't know. He dragged in a deep breath and followed her into the pawn shop.

"Deputy Grayson, where'd you find this pretty little thing?" Big, bald curmudgeon Joe Baumgartner grinned across the counter at Phoebe, holding the ring in his chubby fingers.

Nash couldn't recall a time when Joe smiled, much less grinned. "On the highway. What can you do for her?"

The Joe Nash knew wiped the smile from his face, pulled out a jeweler's loupe and stared down at the ring. "I don't know that I can do much. I'm no expert, but this ain't no diamond. I think it's a cubic zirconia. I'd have to send it to my cousin in Dallas to be sure."

Phoebe's brows dipped. "Cubic zirconia? You're kidding, right?" She focused those pretty green eyes on the old man, tears pooling to make them even greener. "Is it worth *anything*?"

Joe shrugged. "Might be worth twenty-five bucks for the gold."

Nash watched as Phoebe seemed to shrink into her dress, her eyes rounding like a puppy in the animal shelter.

"Is that all?"

The shop owner nodded.

She fingered the locket at her throat. "What about this locket?"

The pawn shop owner shook his head, reached beneath the cabinet, pulled out a tray full of antique lockets and laid it on the counter. "Can't sell the ones I have."

Phoebe's crushed look hit Nash in the gut. Damn. "Is that all you can do, Joe?"

Joe tipped his head, staring at the ring in Phoebe's hand. "Twenty-five is really more than I think I can sell it for." He raised his hands, palms upward. "Take it, or leave it."

"I'll take it," Phoebe said, her voice barely above a whisper.

The pawn shop owner counted out the bills and handed them to Phoebe. "Sorry I couldn't give you more."

She handed him the ring. "You did the best you could. Thank you." Phoebe turned away, her bare feet tripping over the train she'd let fall to the floor.

Nash dove forward, caught her and lifted her in his arms.

Old Joe rounded the counter and helped pile her dress on top of her. "Good luck, missy. Hope that jerk who stiffed you gets what he deserves."

Phoebe shot a wide-eyed glance at Joe and stuttered, "Th-thank you." She wadded the bills in her hand and turned to Nash. "Ready?"

He nodded. As he carried her through the door,

her scent wafted beneath his nose. Nash nearly groaned out loud. He had to get her situated soon.

She leaned down and opened the back door of the SUV.

Nash settled her onto the seat and helped her gather as much of the dress as he could, shoving the folds into the vehicle. Finally, he was able to shut the door, figuring he had maybe five more minutes before Rider arrived with her car in tow. If he could wrap this up quickly, he could have her off his hands sooner rather than later.

Feeling like a chauffeur to the rich, he drove the SUV to the only shoe store in town. Sighing, he got out, opened the back door and waited while she got out, the ridiculous dress swelling around her. If anything, it appeared to be getting bigger.

She tiptoed into the store and crossed to the nearest display of sensible shoes.

Lola, the shoe storeowner, hurried from the back toward Phoebe like a hawk swooping in to claim its prey. When she spotted Nash, she stopped in her tracks, her eyes widening, her dark red lips curling into a smile. "Nash, honey, what can I help you with?" She altered her direction from Phoebe to Nash.

Nash ground his back teeth together.

Though nice enough, Lola had made it clear she had her heart set on Chance, Nash's older brother. Never mind Lola was easily twenty years older than Chance. Her behavior was a constant source of pain for Chance, and he'd told her on more than one occasion he wasn't interested. Unfortunately, Lola refused to take no for an answer.

Lola touched Nash's arm. "Where's that brother of yours?"

"I imagine he's sleeping. He worked last night."

"Mmm." Lola ran her fingers down his chest, tapping the buttons one at a time. "You Grayson men are all so…so…delicious. And men in uniform are so very *hard* to resist." Her hand dropped lower, catching on his belt buckle.

Easing back an inch, he captured her hand before she could get her claws into him. "Lola, could you please help Miss Smith find a pair of shoes? She seems to have left the church without hers."

Lola blinked and turned toward the only other person in the store. "Oh, a customer. How nice of you to bring her to me." She batted her eyelashes up at Nash. "I'm available tonight, if you'd like to show me your…badge."

"Not interested, Lola." He turned her toward Phoebe. "Please, help Miss Smith."

Lola pouted, but pasted a smile on her face. "What can I get you, sweetie?"

Phoebe, her cheeks a rosy shade of pink, pointed at a pair of serviceable boat shoes. "I just need something to wear."

"Oh, honey, those won't go with the dress." Lola

33

plucked a pair of rhinestone-studded stilettos from a display shelf. "How about these?"

"I'm not interested in high heels. I need something I can work in. I need to find a job as soon as possible."

"Oh, dear heart, you can work in any shoes I sell here. It all depends on what kind of work you're interested in."

Phoebe's brows furrowed.

Nash stepped forward. "Lola, she just needs to be able to walk." He lifted a tennis shoe from a display shelf. "What can she get for twenty-five dollars?"

Lola blinked. "Nash, you know I can't discount my inventory that much. I have to pay the rent."

"You don't have anything for under twenty-five?" Nash's hopes of being home in time for dinner were quickly fizzling.

"The only shoes I sell for that price are children's sizes." She glanced at Phoebe's feet and tipped her head. "Your feet are small, but I don't think they're quite *that* small."

Phoebe held out the bills. "I only have twenty-five dollars. I need shoes and something to wear besides this dress, so that I can find a job and a place to stay."

"An admirable goal." Lola tapped a finger to her chin. "There's a thrift store behind the fire station. If you don't mind secondhand clothing, you can make that twenty-five go a lot farther than one pair of my cheapest shoes. And the proceeds from the sales go toward the women's shelter."

Nash shook his head. "I forgot about the thrift store."

"I know how it feels to get out of a bad relationship. At least you got smart before you said I do."

Phoebe gave her a shaky smile.

Lola touched her arm. "Sweetie, I have an apartment over my garage, if you're interested."

Phoebe's face brightened. "I am." Just as quickly, the light faded. "But I don't have any money."

Lola wrapped an arm around her. "I can waive the first month's rent if you're willing to clean it yourself. I've been using it as a place to store Christmas decorations for the shop."

"Thank you." The young bride nodded. "I'll do whatever it takes."

"Good." Lola backed up a step. "Go find some shoes and clothes. I'll have a key for you when you get back."

Nash wasn't so sure he was happy Lola had offered the woman a place to stay. If he had his way, he would have bundled Phoebe onto a bus headed back the way she came. Now it appeared she was staying in town a little longer.

"Come on. We need to get to the thrift shop before they close." Nash grabbed Phoebe's hand. At the contact with her hand, an electric charge raced up his arm. He told himself it was nothing. This woman was a stranger. An almost bride, who'd almost married another man, and probably wasn't staying in Hellfire any longer than it took to figure out the town was too small for her. Most young people moved on, finding the town too cramped and the community too nosey.

Yeah, she'd be gone before the week was out.

No worries, right?

That warm rush of sensations coursing through his veins was in reaction to the hot Texas sun, not the hot little bride holding his hand.

Keep telling yourself that, Nash. Keeping telling yourself. Doing so wouldn't make it true.

CHAPTER 3

As PHOEBE EASED past Deputy Grayson, she caught a whiff of his cologne. No…not really cologne, but the fresh scent of soap, the outdoors and one hundred percent male. No other man she'd been around made her heart skip several beats and then rush into a pounding frenzy.

She was embarrassed, overwrought and afraid of going to jail. At least that was her excuse for the way her breath caught and her pulse pounded whenever the deputy put his hands on her.

In a hurry to move past him, she wasn't paying much attention to the ground at her feet—not that she could see it below the yards of taffeta and tulle. Why had she picked this dress? She missed the step down from the curb, stumbled and felt a sharp stabbing pain in her big toe. "Ouch!" Phoebe's knees buckled. She would have fallen except for the big hand that grabbed her elbow and held her up.

"Are you okay?" Grayson bent over her, his brows knit.

She shook her head and pulled the skirt of her dress away from her foot. Deep red blood dripped onto the bright white of the wedding gown still draped across the ground. "I must have stepped on glass or something."

"Is it still in your foot?" he asked, bending closer to study her bleeding toe. "Well, damn. You can't go bleeding all over town." Once again, he scooped her into his arms.

That familiar scent of him wrapped around her with his arms. Phoebe's heartbeat did that quirky thing of stopping and then pounding hard as if she were racing for a finish line. "I'm so sorry to be such a mess. I didn't think before I left…" She shook her head. Tears welled in her eyes. Before one could drop, she glanced away, refusing to appear weak in front of such a strong, virile man. If she wanted to be independent, she sure as hell had to start acting like it. "Put me down. I can manage."

"The hell you can." He juggled her body and opened the back door to the SUV, setting her on the seat. Then he pointed a finger. "Stay." Before she could respond, he turned toward the rear of the vehicle and opened the hatch.

"I'm not a dog," Phoebe grumbled. Just like her

father, the deputy had given her a command and expected her to follow it. If she weren't bleeding and barefoot, she'd get her ass out of the back of Grayson's vehicle and march right out of his life. But she was bleeding...and barefoot. As Grayson appeared, Phoebe's stomach rumbled loudly. And hungry.

It didn't seem possible, but the deputy's frown deepened. "How long has it been since you've eaten?"

Phoebe didn't want to think about food. She had a dead fiancé in the trunk of a stolen car. An even louder burble sounded from her belly. Pressing a hand to the tight wedding dress, she shrugged. "Yesterday evening at the rehearsal dinner," she answered, although she hadn't really touched the expensive filet mignon the chef prepared for her and the rest of her bridal party.

Sitting at the table with Ryan on one side and her father on the other, her mother across the table from her, laughing and flirting with one of her father's business partners, Phoebe had experienced a wave of panic. Her stomach knotted and her hands clenched in her lap. She was marrying a man her father had selected. A man she'd dated and kissed several times, but she really didn't know. How had she let this happen?

"Hey, it's not all that bad. Just a little cut." Deputy Grayson glanced up from the first-aid kit he laid on the ground.

Phoebe bit her bottom lip to keep it from trembling. So much for being tough and independent. "I'm okay. Really."

"Trying to convince me?" He glanced up, his mouth quirking upward on one corner. "Or yourself?"

She laughed, though it sounded more like a sob. "Ever have one of those days that goes wrong in so many ways your head spins?"

He snorted. "As a sheriff's deputy and a ranch owner, yes. More often than you can imagine."

Phoebe stared down at the top of his cowboy hat as he bent to open the first aid kit. "You own a ranch?"

He nodded, extracting an alcohol prep pad. "My brothers and I own a ranch close to town. We run cattle and horses."

"And you're a deputy?"

He shrugged and tore open the packet. "I like to keep busy since coming home from the war." He lifted her foot in one of his big hands and studied the cut. "I don't see anything embedded in the wound."

Phoebe wiggled her toes. "I can't feel any."

"This might sting a little." He touched the alcohol-soaked pad to the pad of her toe.

A sharp flash of pain ripped through her toe. Phoebe instinctively gasped and jerked back her foot.

Grayson held her foot firmly in his hand and waited for her to relax. "Ready?"

She braced herself and nodded. "Just do it."

He cleaned the wound and applied a sterile bandage. Then he tucked her into the back of the vehicle. "Let's find some shoes, before you cut another toe." He closed the door, effectively locking her in the SUV.

Phoebe sat in the back seat, her foot and leg tingling from the deputy's gentle touch. Shoes, clothes and then she had to find a way to get out of Hellfire. The deputy was proving to be far too attractive. For a woman who should have been married by now, she was having highly inappropriate thoughts about a virtual stranger.

The handsome deputy stowed the kit in the back of the vehicle and climbed into the driver's seat. Without a word, he drove a couple blocks, turned and parked in front of another building.

Phoebe grabbed the door handle and tried to open it, remembering at the last minute it was locked.

He opened it. Instead of backing away to let her get out on her own, he bent and lifted her into his arms.

Rather than argue, Phoebe draped an arm around his neck and sighed. As soon as she had a pair of shoes, she could get around on her own. She didn't need this man's arms to carry her everywhere. Though they were solid, and muscular, and so very strong...

He backed through the door and carried her inside. "Peg, I have a customer for you."

A small, athletic woman with graying strawberry blond hair leaned out from a rack of blue jeans. "Oh, hi, Nash." She blinked, doing a double-take. "What on earth have you got there? Did I not get an invite to the wedding?" She grinned.

Nash's jaw tightened. "I picked up this stray on the highway into town. I don't suppose you could help her find some shoes to fit?"

Phoebe frowned. "I'm not a stray, and I can speak for myself." She glared up at him. "Please, put me down."

He set her on her feet. "You're in capable hands. Peg will help you with whatever you need."

With her weight balanced on her good foot, Phoebe gathered her dress around her. "Thank you." She turned her attention to a large room with row upon row of clothes racks and felt overwhelmed. "Oh, dear, where should I start?"

Peg's smile disappeared. "Sweetheart, let me help you." She held out her hand. "Margaret Clayton. Most folks around here call me Peg."

Phoebe took her hand. "Phoebe…S-Smith." She glanced around. "I need shoes and clothes I can work in." She held out the bills in her hand. "Whatever I can get for twenty-five dollars."

Peg curled her hand around Phoebe's without taking the money. "Honey, you keep your money.

This thrift shop supports the women's shelter. From the looks of you, I'd say you could use a little of that support right now." She hooked a hand in the crook of Phoebe's elbow and herded her toward a rack of clothes.

For the first time since he'd come across Phoebe on the side of the road, Nash was more than four feet away from her. As soon as she left his side, he felt a void where she'd been. When he should have been breathing a sigh of relief and stepping outside into the fresh Texas air, he stood rooted to the tile floor, wondering what the hell was wrong with him. Rescuing a damsel in distress must have triggered some kind of residual protective instinct. That had to be it. He pushed his hat back on his head, semi-satisfied with his reasoning.

Then why hadn't he had the same feeling when he'd rescued Maggie Parker from her abusive boyfriend? She was young and as pretty as Phoebe. Maggie was a friend. He knew her and he didn't know Phoebe. Yet, he hadn't felt this weird sense of territorial claim or belonging he was feeling toward the runaway bride who kept looking back, as if afraid he'd leave her stranded in the thrift shop.

Nash spun on his boot heels and started for the exit and clear, country air. He had his hand on the door when he made the mistake of looking over his shoulder.

Peg had disappeared in the maze of clothes racks.

Phoebe stood with her wedding dress bunched in her arms, her gaze on him, her eyes round and scared.

Damn.

Instead of pushing through the door, he stopped, turned his back to the windows and leaned against the doorframe, crossing his arms as if he had all day to wait for Phoebe to get dressed in something besides that billowing poof of a wedding dress. He nodded toward her, keeping his face set and serious.

Phoebe's shoulders relaxed, and she turned toward Peg, who approached with an armload of denim.

"Start with these. I guessed your size." She was back in a moment with blouses of all shapes and colors. Like a child's automated toy, Peg darted left and right, ducking in and out of racks, until she had a shopping cart filled with a mound of clothing and another filled with shoes.

At the sight, Nash groaned and chanced a glance at his watch. He keyed his mic and spoke into the radio on his shoulder. "Gretchen, could you notify the office I'll be delayed another thirty minutes to an hour?"

"Sure, honey. Any problems? Need backup?"

Did he need backup? Hell yeah! A runaway bride, whose gaze could melt him in his tracks, was something he had never come up against. And by against... her warm, curvy body pressed to his had left a definite impression. "No. I don't need backup," he said, his voice a little harsher than he'd intended. He didn't need backup. He needed someone else to take over so he could run as far away as possible.

Hell. And that really wasn't an option. Not when she finally emerged from the dressing room wearing a pair of slim-fitting jeans that clung to her body like a second skin. Those and a pale green, short-sleeved sweater that hugged the rounded swell of her breasts and narrow waist had Nash shifting in his boots, wishing he could adjust the fit of his trousers to accommodate what the sight of her was doing to his libido.

Sweet Jesus!

In the wedding dress, she was a tiny fairy princess enveloped in clouds of poofy cotton candy. In the jeans, light green sweater, and a pair of gently scuffed, brown cowboy boots she was the girl next door, only better and somehow more real. She'd pulled the remaining pins and her long auburn hair fell around her shoulders in wild waves.

When she turned her gaze to meet his, Nash's breath caught and held.

Alarm bells rang out in his head. *Warning! Warning!* Had he listened, he'd have run the other way. Peg would have seen that Phoebe got a ride to Lola's apartment or the women's shelter. Nash had no obligation to stick around and see her to her next destination.

His feet wouldn't budge from the floor. He couldn't breathe, much less move when she gazed at him with those eyes the soft green of spring hay.

Peg held out a bag bulging with other items of clothing and another with several pairs of shoes. When Phoebe extended the twenty-five dollars, Peg lifted her hand and shook her head. "Take them. Pay it forward when you get on your feet."

"Thank you so very much," Phoebe said. "I'll pay you back as soon as I can."

"What do you want me to do with the wedding dress?" Peg asked, tilting her head toward the dressing room.

"Keep it, sell it, or burn it. I have no use for the thing."

"Consider it payment for the items you're taking with you." Peg smiled. "I'm sure it more than covers them. And you look wonderful and ready to take on life on your own terms."

Phoebe hugged Peg and turned to Nash, her eyes swimming with unshed tears. "I'm ready." She squared her shoulders, even as her bottom lip trembled. She sucked it between her teeth and lifted her chin.

He swallowed past the tightening in his throat and resisted the urge to gather Phoebe in his arms, to protect her from the world and feel this whole new woman, free of the wedding dress, pressed against his body. But resist, he did. To hold her now would start a landslide of something he was sure would bury him completely. One thing was certain, he wouldn't emerge unscathed. Outside the thrift shop, he held the SUV door for Phoebe.

She slid in, drawing in her slim legs like a celebrity, or someone used to riding in the back seat of a limousine.

Nash blinked. That thought tugged at his memory. With her hair down and that ridiculous dress gone, she appeared somewhat familiar. He'd seen that face before, but he couldn't put his finger on where. "Should I know you?"

Her eyes widened, and she turned away. "I don't see how. We just met today."

His gaze narrowed, as if by squinting he could pinpoint that memory of where he'd seen her before. For a long moment, he stared at her profile. Finally, he shook his head. "Guess I'm mistaken."

"Yes," she said, her voice breathy. "Perhaps so."

He shut the door, rounded the vehicle to the driver's side and climbed in. He glanced at her in the rearview mirror. "Were you at the last rodeo in Fort Worth?"

Phoebe shook her head and stared out the window, fingering the locket at her throat. "No."

"Where are you from?" he asked, surprised he hadn't asked before. What kind of deputy was he, anyway?

"Does it matter?" She continued to stare out the

window, allowing a long strand of hair to swing forward and block her eyes from his view. "I'm sure you have better things to do than chauffeur me around. Likely Lola will be waiting for my return."

A non-answer. Nash's eyes narrowed. He supposed she wasn't in a hurry to let her folks know where she'd run to, nor did she want a well-meaning sheriff's deputy to notify her family of her whereabouts.

Nash shifted into reverse, backing out of the parking lot. Two minutes later, he pulled into the parking lot of Lola's shoe store.

Lola hurried out, locked the door behind her and held up a key. "I have the key to the apartment."

"Good." Just a few more minutes and he could wash his hands of the runaway bride. Nash tipped his cowboy hat at the older woman. He turned in the driver's seat, and tilted his head toward the rear of the vehicle where Phoebe sat. "Do you want to ride in the back, or take your own vehicle?"

"Any other time, I'd die for a chance to ride in the backseat of your squad car." She winked at Nash. "I have to get back fairly quickly. I'm expecting a delivery at any time. But I'll take a rain check if you promise to use the handcuffs."

Nash shook his head. "Lola, you know I can't play with the cuffs. They're for real police business."

Lola pouted. "I could pretend to be a lady of the evening, and you could arrest me for soliciting." She plumped her ample breasts, the girls nearly spilling out of her tight sweater and the bra that could barely contain them. "I'll even let you frisk me."

Nash tried not to smile and thus encourage the woman's naughty behavior. "As tempting as that sounds, I have to decline. Besides, I thought you liked fire fighters better."

"Oh, I do. They are so very...hot." She fanned her cheek with her hand. "But lawmen are a close second."

Phoebe's gaze shot from Lola to Nash and back during the entire exchange.

Nash sighed. The bride would wonder what she was getting into with Hellfire's infamous Lola. The middle-aged woman loved to flirt. Since her husband passed away and left her with a comfortable insurance stipend, she enjoyed playing the field and hitting on all the single young men and some of the older men in town. Sometimes she was annoying, but mostly she was harmless. Just lonely.

Nash drove the few short blocks, parked in front of Lola's house, got out and opened the door for Phoebe.

Phoebe climbed out, and stared at the pretty charcoal-gray craftsman-style cottage with a detached garage set back at the end of a long driveway.

Lola zoomed up the street in a bright orange Corvette, skidding to a stop in the driveway. She jumped out and held out a key. "What do you think of the place?"

"I love your house," Phoebe said.

"I kind of like it too." Lola smiled. "Come on. You might not like the apartment as much. I haven't been in it since Christmas. I'm not sure how big a mess it is."

"I can handle it," Phoebe said, determined to make it work. With no other option presenting itself and no money to live on, she had to take what she could get.

"If you want to work for me as a housekeeper, I could use help once a week. The shop keeps me pretty busy."

Nash cleared his throat. "If you are comfortable with Miss Lola, I'm off duty and need to check in at the station."

Phoebe drew her bottom lip between her teeth and stared up into his eyes. "Thank you so much for all you've done. I hope I can repay your kindness some day."

He tipped his cowboy hat, suddenly reluctant to leave her, but he didn't have a reason to stay. "Not necessary. It's part of my job." Nodding to Lola, he gave her a brief smile. "Let me know if you two need anything. You know how to get a hold of me."

With that, he turned and hurried away. Yes, he wanted to stay and make sure Phoebe was settled into the garage apartment, but she wasn't his responsibility and the more he was around her, the more he wanted to stay with her. Not good. Not good at all.

He wasn't in the market for a girlfriend and though she said she wasn't going back to where she came from, there wasn't much in Hellfire to keep her here. He was better off walking away.

Almost to the SUV, he reached for the door handle when footsteps crunched on the gravel and a soft voice stopped him.

"Deputy Grayson?"

He turned to stare down into those soft green eyes, his pulse ratcheting up. "Yes, Miss Smith?"

"Thank you." She touched his arm. "And no matter what happens, I promise I'm not a bad person." She flung her arms around his neck and kissed his cheek. Then she turned and ran back to where Lola stood, a grin stretching the older woman's dark lipstick-covered mouth.

Warmth rushed through Nash and tingling spread from where Phoebe's lips had touched his cheek. He raised a hand to the spot and stared at the woman, a frown pulling his brows downward.

He hadn't begun the day with the intent of finding a runaway bride stranded on the side of the road. Scenarios like that were only found in those unrealistic romance novels women liked reading. No. He hadn't asked for a kiss. But now that she'd done it, she couldn't undo it, and he couldn't unfeel it.

Nash gave a curt nod, turned and fought to keep

from leaping into his SUV, though he knew running away wouldn't get him away from the haunting look of the pretty redhead with the eyes the color of the soft green moss.

In the few short hours he'd known Phoebe Smith, she'd crawled beneath his defenses.

Damn.

So distracted by the kiss he couldn't think straight, Nash pulled out of Lola's drive without looking and almost backed into a black four-door sedan that had slowed on the street in front of Lola's house. When Nash finally glanced in the rearview mirror, he slammed his foot on the brake, stopping the big SUV mere inches from the sedan.

The driver must have been shaken by the near-miss, because he goosed his accelerator and peeled off a layer of his tires on the hot Texas pavement, screaming away from Nash's vehicle.

Nash slammed his palm against the steering wheel. "Damn!" How could he be so careless? He gave himself a firm shake, looked both ways, with one last glance at the two women staring from halfway down the driveway and pulled into the empty street. Phoebe Smith was a distraction he could not afford. Not now. Or ever. He'd been down that twisted path before and it only led to heartbreak.

CHAPTER 4

WHEN DEPUTY GRAYSON pulled out of the driveway, Phoebe's heart clenched in her chest. He'd been the rock in her extremely turbulent day. Though he didn't know half of what she'd gone through, and had yet to deal with, he'd seen that she got the proper clothing and shoes, met a woman who could put her up in her own apartment and he'd even doctored her cut toe.

Maybe she was putting him up on a white horse, with the halo-effect of a knight in shining armor, but she had been so grateful for the help when she'd needed it most. Unfortunately, the one person who'd helped her most would also be the one who'd ultimately arrest her and charge her with murder once his brother opened the trunk of the rental car and discovered the body of her fiancé.

What had made her run after the deputy, she didn't know. But as he'd walked away, Phoebe couldn't let him go without telling him what his actions meant to her. And the kiss...

It was only a kiss on the cheek. Nothing more than a woman would give a father or brother. Though the feelings she'd had when Grayson had held her in his arms were anything but sisterly.

When he'd nearly backed into the dark sedan, Phoebe stifled a scream. She let go of the breath caught in her throat when the sedan sped away and the deputy pulled out of the drive. Pressing a hand to her chest in a useless attempt to slow her thundering pulse, she sucked in a deep breath and released it slowly.

"Nash is quite the heartthrob, isn't he?" a voice said beside her.

Phoebe turned to face Lola, shocked she'd forgotten the woman was even there. "I'm sorry?"

"Nash." Lola nodded toward the disappearing SUV. "Deputy Grayson." She grinned. "His first name is Nash. He's one of the four Grayson brothers. Every last one of them is tall, dark and so handsome they'll make your panties damp."

Heat rose in Phoebe's cheeks at Lola's words, and her belly clenched. She'd met two of the four and knew at least half of the truth of what Lola was saying. "There are four of them?"

Lola nodded, her gaze also following the sheriff deputy's vehicle. "I'd give my left breast to be twenty years younger." She sighed. "But I always say, I might be weathered, but this old hearth still has a scorching flame burning inside." With a shrug, she sighed. "And it doesn't hurt to flirt." With a wink, she turned toward the garage apartment. "If you don't like the place, I can put you up in my spare bedroom until you find something you like better."

"I'll just be happy to have a roof over my head." And as soon as she could find Rider Grayson's auto repair shop, she'd do something about getting rid of the body in the trunk of the rental car.

Lola led the way up the stairs and unlocked the door of the garage apartment. Inside were stacks of cardboard boxes, plastic containers and strands of colored lights. "When my husband was alive, we rented out the apartment. After he passed and our tenant moved out, I didn't want to fool with it."

Phoebe turned to Lola, her heart constricting. "Oh. I'm so sorry for your loss."

Lola gave her a gentle smile with her bright red lips. The brightness of her gaze dimmed a little. "It's been five years, and not a day goes by that I don't think of him. He was my everything—my soulmate. But he made me promise that if anything happened to him, I shouldn't stop loving life and I should get on with living. Maybe find me another man to fill my days and heart." She snorted. "I haven't found one who gets me like George did." She winked. "But I'm trying. I've had my sights set on the Grayson boys."

Phoebe's chest pinched and she frowned. She didn't have any hold over Nash Grayson. But the thought of any other woman with him made her fingers curl into fists. She glanced down at her bunched hands, perplexed. She'd never felt that way about Ryan. Nor had she felt like Lola felt about her dead husband. Ryan had been a man her father and mother had chosen for her.

Being the dutiful daughter, whose peers had all landed successful matches, Phoebe had let the wave of her familial obligations sweep her along. And where had that gotten her? In a relationship she regretted and now facing a potential murder rap. She really needed to get to the auto repair shop as soon as possible.

Lola led the way into the apartment chatting all the way.

Phoebe followed, barely hearing a word the woman said until she stepped through the door.

"The nice thing about living here is that you're only a couple blocks from the sheriff's office and fire station." Lola's lips curled into a secretive smile. "And you know what that means."

Phoebe came back to the present with a frown. "No. What does that mean?" Other than it wouldn't take long for a deputy to get there once they found the body in the trunk of the rental car. A cool chill rippled across her skin.

"The fire fighters arrive in less than three minutes, if you have an emergency."

"You know this because…?" Phoebe queried.

Lola glanced toward the sky. "You could say I've had an emergency or two." She spun to face Phoebe. "They're like clockwork. Three minutes on the dot." With a quick glance around, she grimaced. "It is a mess, but the bed is somewhere in the corner and a small balcony juts off the back if you get claustrophobic. I think the former owners had the apartment made up for their grown son as a weaning off option before he got a place of his own. When it's not full of junk, the space is kind of cozy. You have your own kitchenette and small refrigerator, if you can find them."

"I'm sure I'll be fine." Phoebe tried not to think of the cobwebs hanging from the rafters. And, really, how hard could it be to knock down a few spider webs or clean up a little dust? Lots of people did it. Phoebe shivered. As the daughter of a very wealthy man, she'd never had to clean her own room. Even in college, her father had hired a maid to clean her apartment.

Straightening her shoulders, she told herself it would be an adventure, a chance to learn and grow as a person free of her parents' expectations. She could do this.

"As for the boxes, I suppose you could move them to the garage. I'd help, but I have a ton of new inventory I'm sorting through at the shop. I need to get it on the shelves as soon as possible."

"Oh." Phoebe turned to Lola. "Do you need help? I can deal with this at another time."

Lola patted Phoebe's arm. "You need to stay here and find the bed. I'm sure that it'll take a little time pulling off the dustcovers. Open the windows and let in some sunlight and fresh air. I'll bring up fresh sheets before I head back to the shop."

Lola left her standing among the stacks of boxes, all of her worldly goods crammed into a couple of plastic bags and the pathetic twenty-five dollars wadded in her jeans pocket. The task of moving, sorting and cleaning seemed overwhelming. After all the other things she'd been through that day, cleaning was a minor inconvenience. She could stand there feeling sorry for herself, or get to work and make some sense out of her life.

She changed into a slightly faded T-shirt from her bag of clothes and went to work moving boxes from the apartment down to the garage. By the time she'd made her way through fifteen of them, she was cursing her personal trainer for insisting on spin class instead of the stair climber. Her hamstrings were screaming, and her back hurt like it never hurt before. The kicker was that she considered herself in fairly good shape. If she ever went back to that gym in Fort Worth, she'd be sure to ask for a refund of her father's money.

All the while Phoebe worked, she waited for the shoe to drop and Ryan's body to be discovered. Every time she heard a siren, she tensed and waited for the wailing to swing her way and stop in the gravel driveway of Lola's house.

Good to her word, Lola had delivered a set of clean sheets, towels and a couple sampler bottles of shampoo and body wash that looked like the kind hotels offered their guests. By the time the sun dropped below the horizon, Phoebe was hot, sweaty, and physically and mentally exhausted.

She had a pretty good path through to the kitchenette and could squeeze past old furniture she couldn't lift to get to the tiny bathroom and shower. Though the window air conditioner worked, the old unit had struggled to cool the small apartment in the heat of the Texas summer afternoon.

Too tired to care how small the shower stall was, Phoebe stripped out of the dirty clothing and stepped beneath the spray, shocked by the chill of the water. Apparently, the water heater wasn't working or hadn't been turned on. But after a moment or two, the cold water felt great against her sweat-soaked skin.

Once she stepped out of the shower, she almost

felt human. Dressed in a clean pair of jeans, a dark blouse and a pair of gently worn running shoes, she exited the apartment, so hungry she couldn't think straight. First, she'd find food and then the auto repair shop where the rental car had been taken. If she was lucky, Rider hadn't searched the trunk for a spare. If she was even luckier, the tire would be magically intact and inflated. She'd be able to drive the rental car away to dispose of Ryan's body or ditch the car somewhere and walk back to her new life in Hellfire.

A cold sense of dread chilled her in the early evening gloom. How had Ryan ended up in that trunk? He hadn't fallen in and suffered a heart attack. The man had been fit, active and too young for clogged arteries. Which indicated someone had offed him and shoved him into the trunk.

Guilt tore at Phoebe. She was upset at her fiancé's demise. But not heartbroken. Sure, she felt awful that he was dead. But her sense of relief that she didn't have to marry him was just as strong. Still, she hadn't wished him dead. Just unavailable to marry her. God, was she becoming a cold-hearted bitch like her mother could be? Leaving that world behind had been the best decision she could have made. But with no money, no identification and no prospects of a job, she was navigating uncharted waters and afraid she would be swept under.

She walked two blocks to Main Street, passing by

quaint little mom-and-pop stores, finally coming across Bob's Diner. The undeniable scent of food wafting out of the establishment almost brought Phoebe to her knees. With the last bit of her waning strength, she pushed open the door and entered, her mouthwatering.

"Sit where you like," a female voice called out.

Phoebe glanced around at the black-and-white checkered floor, shiny red booth seats and chrome bar and managed to stagger to an empty booth in the far right corner. She reached for the laminated menu wedged between the napkin holder and the salt and pepper shakers and stared at the array of potential entrees, her stomach aching with the need for nourishment.

"Honey, what can I getcha?" A middle-aged waitress, dressed in a fifties-style, pink skirt and top, bobby socks, saddle shoes and a ribbon holding her hair back, stopped next to her table. "The meatloaf is fresh out of the oven and one of Bob's best."

"Sounds wonderful." With only twenty-five dollars to last until she landed a job, she had to be sparing with her money, something completely new to her lifestyle. "But I'd rather have the grilled cheese sandwich and a glass of tap water." She set the menu back where she'd found it and smiled up at the waitress. If she was very careful, she might make the little bit of money last until the end of the week, at which time she'd better have a plan in place to get more, or she'd starve.

"Are you the young woman who moved into Lola's garage?"

Her cheeks heating, Phoebe nodded.

"Word gets around in small towns." The waitress grinned, wiped her hand on the white apron covering her pink skirt and held it out. "Judy Johnson."

Phoebe took the other woman's hand. "Phoebe Smith. Nice to meet you."

"Let me know if you need anything. Most everyone knows everyone else, and we help each other out. 'Specially when they're down and out."

Phoebe couldn't help but feel a little embarrassed. She'd never had to worry about money, and she'd never had to ask for help. She glanced around the diner. "You wouldn't happen to know anyone who might be hiring, would you? I need a job."

"What kind of experience do you have?" Judy asked.

Experience? Hell, she'd never held a job. With a degree in home economics, she wasn't sure how her coursework would translate to anything there in Hellfire. She shook her head. "I don't have any experience."

The waitress frowned and touched her chin. "I'd say apply here, but Bob's got all the wait staff he needs." She tilted her head and stared at the far left corner of the building, tapping her chin. Finally, she straightened, her eyes widening. "How about the Ugly Stick Saloon?"

"Ugly Stick Saloon?" What kind of place had a name like that?

"Sure! Audrey Anderson owns it. Only thing is it's out on the county line. You got a car?"

Phoebe almost answered yes, until she remembered the car she had was a rental she didn't own, and a dead man occupied the trunk. Her shoulders slumped, along with her hopes. "No."

Judy tapped the end of her pen to her chin. "Hmm. There's always the chance one of the other waitresses could give you a ride if your shifts match." She wrote a number on her order pad and ripped off a page. "Here's her phone number. It's worth giving her a call. Audrey always needs waitresses and the tips are good. A lot better than here." She winked. "I'd work there myself, but I'm getting too old for the late nights."

Phoebe folded the paper and slipped it into her jeans pocket. She'd give this Audrey person a call when she found a phone she could use for free.

Judy had turned and walked a few steps when she spun back around. "In case you don't have a phone, you can use the one on the counter." She walked away, pointing at the phone as she passed it on her way to the kitchen with Phoebe's order.

The waitress's smile was so warm and friendly Phoebe's throat thickened and her eyes stung.

So far, the people she'd met in Hellfire had bent over backward to help her. Would they be as open and friendly if they knew what was in the trunk of the rental car?

Phoebe pushed back her shoulders and stood. She'd just have to make sure they didn't find out. And if she could get a job at the Ugly Stick Saloon, she might not have to get in touch with her father to have him or her mother send her wallet with her identification. She could request it from the DMV and avoid letting her family know where she was until she was good and ready to reveal her location. Hopefully, after she proved she could live on her own, without her father's money or connections.

With her newfound freedom and independence stiffening her backbone, she marched to the counter, lifted the phone and entered the phone number for Audrey Anderson.

After only one ring, a female voice answered. "This is Audrey."

Never having interviewed for a job, much less over the phone, Phoebe's brain froze, and she struggled to come up with an introduction. Finally, she said, "Hi, I'm Phoebe."

Audrey chuckled, the sound warm and friendly. "Well, Phoebe, what can I do for you?"

She glanced around the diner, her gaze meeting Judy's.

The waitress smiled again and nodded.

Those gestures gave Phoebe the courage to forge on. "I'm new in town, and I was wondering if you needed any help at the..." what was the name of the place?

"At the Ugly Stick?" Audrey assisted. "As a matter of fact, I'm short two waitresses tonight. I'm filling in for one of them, but I could use another. Talk about great timing. Do you own a pair of denim cut-offs?"

Frayed cut-offs had been one of the items Peg had insisted she select. Phoebe answered, "Yes."

"Can you be here in an hour?"

Audrey didn't waste time. "I could, if I could get a ride from Hellfire."

"No problem. My husband is headed this way about then, he can give you a lift, and I can bring you back to town after we close."

"That would be wonderful." Phoebe hugged the phone to her ear, tears welling in her eyes. "Thank you so much."

"No," Audrey said. "Thank you! We'll be swamped tonight with the tri-county rodeo going on. This will be a *big* help to me."

Phoebe provided the address of her garage apartment. Audrey stated her husband, Jackson, had business in Hellfire anyway, and would be there in forty-five minutes. After she hung up, Phoebe returned to her table where Judy had set a glass of water.

Minutes later, the waitress brought her food.

The golden toasted grilled cheese sandwich looked better than any of the high-dollar chef-prepared dinners she'd eaten in the past. So hungry she could barely see straight, she wolfed down the sandwich and the potato chips that accompanied it, paid for her meal and hugged Judy on her way out the door.

Going from homeless and broke, with nothing more than the wedding dress on her back, she now had an apartment, a job and a full stomach. Life was looking up. As she left Bob's Diner, she looked both ways on Main Street, wondering which way she should go to get to Rider Grayson's auto repair shop. With thirty minutes to spare before Jackson arrived at her apartment to drive her to the Ugly Stick Saloon, she had time to find the auto shop and maybe buy a few groceries. Removing the body would have to wait until after the town of Hellfire went to sleep. Then she'd have to start her life of crime by breaking and entering into the auto shop and figuring out how to move the body of a one-hundred-eighty-pound man.

Phoebe wondered if her personal trainer had a program for heavy lifting for the criminally inclined. Though she found nothing humorous in her situation, she couldn't help a bark of laughter as she wandered through the streets of Hellfire.

Finally, she came to a building with Grayson's Auto Repairs written in bold lettering on a sign positioned over the door. The only light inside came from a single bulb shining in the back of the building.

A dark sedan drove by on the street behind her, slowing as it approached where Phoebe stood.

She hunched her shoulders and continued down the sidewalk. In a small town, everyone knew or wanted to know everyone else's business. If she stood too long in front of a building, she'd draw attention. Oh, hell, who was she kidding? The new girl in town would draw attention no matter what. Phoebe walked on.

The sedan kept pace. After a few steps, tingling spread down Phoebe's spine. Had her father's bodyguards or private investigators caught up with her? She walked faster. At the next corner, she made a quick left, ducking onto a street with only one street light halfway down the block.

Before the sedan had a chance to make that same turn, Phoebe sprinted to the end of a commercial building and turned into the back alley. As soon as she did, it was as if the light had been snuffed. Using only the moonlight and the distant and somewhat sporadic lights from nearby homes, she hurried through a maze of trash bins and pallet stacks. Footsteps behind her made her move faster, until she was running, leaping and stumbling over the obstacles in her path. Finally, she threw herself between a large metal rubbish container and the brick wall of a building.

Her breathing came in swift, shallow breaths, as she strained past the noise of her pulse pounding against her eardrums, and listened for the footsteps. By the sound of it, two people hurried her way, accompanied by an occasional curse and a loud crash as one or both of her pursuers crashed into some hidden object.

Hunkering low in the shadows, she hid and waited, praying the two would pass her by and abandon their search. The low tones of their voices indicated they were men. One paused on the other side of the container.

"Where did she go?" he whispered.

"How the hell do I know?" the other guy said. "I can't see a damned thing."

"Get moving. We have to find her," the first guy said, moving farther away.

Phoebe waited a few more minutes before poking her head out of her hiding place. Her vision had adjusted to the deep gloom. Nothing moved in the alley except a stray cat casually strolling through as if nothing scared him.

Turning back the way she'd come, she hurried toward the rear of the auto repair shop and pressed her nose to the window, peering through the dingy glass. She could make out a couple cars with hoods open and parts lying on the floor of the shop.

God, she hoped Rider hadn't found the body in the trunk. She suspected that whoever chased her down the alley had something to do with the body in the trunk. The only reason they would want her was because she must know Ryan was in there.

Then again, she hadn't seen the men who'd killed him. Which led back to the question of why had they killed Ryan, and why would they now be after her?

CHAPTER 5

"You should have seen old Nash carrying the pretty bride around like he was marching her over a threshold." Rider lifted the beer in his hand. "Never thought I'd see him with a bride. He's too cantankerous to get married. Suppose I'll have to be content with that image. It's probably as close as he'll get to a bride of his own."

"I'm sitting at the table, dumbass," Nash said, tossing back the whiskey shooter he'd ordered, following it with a longneck bottle of his favorite beer. They'd gathered at the Ugly Stick Saloon for a drink after work to celebrate their brother Chance's thirty-first birthday. "You don't have to talk about me like I'm in another county."

Rider clapped a hand on his shoulder. "Sorry, old man. I can't help it. I wish you could have seen it like I did. The look on your face cracked me up!" He laughed again and wiped the tears from his eyes before taking another long draw from his beer.

"I wouldn't push him too hard," Beckett, Nash's oldest brother, said. "He's younger than you, and what do you have to show for yourself? You haven't even come close to landing a girlfriend, much less a wife."

Rider frowned. "I haven't been looking. Besides, we aren't all as old as you, Beckett. You're lucky Kinsey came back to town, or you'd be as single as the rest of us."

Becket's lips curled in a contented smile, and he reached for his fiancée's hand. "I am lucky she came back to town."

"Damn right, you are," Kinsey declared. "But we're not here to talk about the new girl in town, as interesting as she sounds. We're here to celebrate." She lifted her beer. "Happy birthday, Chance."

The other brothers lifted their drinks and echoed Kinsey's sentiment. "Happy birthday!"

After taking a long pull on their drinks, the brothers lowered them and stared around at each other.

"Thirty-one, huh?" Rider clapped Chance on the back. "So when are you settling down and getting married? Seems we need to get busy populating the family tree with little Graysons."

"We can leave that to Beckett and Kinsey." Chance

shook his head. "I'm not in a hurry to find a ball and chain. I like being footloose."

"That's Chance-speak for I can't get a date, and I don't give enough of a damn to figure out why," Rider said. "What we need is an online dating service so we can meet women."

Chance raised his hand. "No way. I prefer to find my own."

Nash agreed with Chance. Online dating wasn't for him, either.

Rider's brows rose. "And how's that working for you, Chance, old man?"

With a shrug, Chance took another swig of his beer, keeping silent.

"Want me to get you boys another round of drinks?" Kinsey glanced around. "Seems Audrey is short some waitresses tonight."

"Bad night to be short, what with the rodeo in town."

"I'm surprised Jackson isn't here to help," Kinsey said as she glanced around. "He's always here on big nights."

Jackson Gray Wolf emerged from the doorway behind the bar with someone behind him. About that time, Kinsey shifted, blocking Nash's view.

Chance gave a low whistle. "Hey, who's the hot redhead with Jackson?"

Nash craned his neck, unable to see past Kinsey. Chance's mention of a redhead had Nash's every nerve on alert. Surely it wasn't the pretty Phoebe he'd rescued on the side of the road earlier that day.

Rider leaned sideways and gave a hoot of laughter. "Well, I'll be damned. It's her!" He glanced at Nash. "Your pretty bride came looking for you, Nash. Whatcha gonna do?"

"She didn't come looking for me." Nash scooted back his chair, in an attempt to get a look at the woman with Jackson, without appearing too interested. He'd never hear the end of the teasing from his brothers.

"You know I could hold off making the repairs to her tire if you want to take a shot at asking her for a date," Rider said.

"I'm not going to date her. She just broke up with her fiancé." Kinsey finally moved, and Nash got a full view of the woman. She wore an Ugly Stick Saloon tank top similar to the ones the other waitresses did, and she'd changed into denim cut-offs that showcased long, slender, toned legs he could imagine wrapped around his waist. She'd combed the riotous curls and secured them in a French braid at the back of her head. He liked her better with her hair loose and crazy around her face. "I doubt she's interested in starting another relationship so soon," he muttered.

Rider's grin widened. "So you admit it. You thought about it, didn't you?"

"Not once," Nash responded, refusing to give

Rider the satisfaction of knowing he was right. Yeah, Nash had thought about asking her out. But the fact she'd run away from her own wedding should be a bright red flag where Phoebe Smith was concerned. She'd left her fiancé at the altar. If she'd done it once, she might do it again. Not that Nash would ask her to marry him. But she was interesting...and beautiful...

No. His fingers tightened on the bottle. Nash wasn't interested in a woman who couldn't make up her mind before such a huge event as a wedding. He almost felt sorry for the schmuck she left behind.

"Well, if you're not asking her out, then I will." Rider pushed to his feet and started for the bar and Phoebe.

Nash hooked his finger in Rider's belt and yanked him back into his chair.

"Hey." Rider glared at him.

With a nod toward Phoebe, who was lifting a tray full of beer bottles and whiskey shooters, Nash said, "Looks like she'll be working for Audrey. Give her a break on her first night."

Phoebe held the tray in front of her, the beer bottles teetering as she worked her way across the floor under the weight.

"Hey, Audrey, who's the new girl?" a man called out.

Audrey smiled and shouted above the noise of the juke box and the men all talking at once. "Everyone say hello to Phoebe. She's new in town and new to the Ugly Stick. Give her a big howdy."

Cowboys raised their hats and everyone in the saloon shouted as one, "Howdy!"

Phoebe's cheeks turned a bright red as she arrived at a table full of dusty men, fresh from the rodeo. One by one, she set bottles on the table. With only one left in the middle of the tray, she reached for it at the same time as one of the men pinched her ass. Phoebe jumped, squealed and lost control of the tray. The last full beer bottle slid sideways and tipped into the lap of the man who'd pinched her.

Nash was out of his chair and halfway across the room before he realized he'd even moved. But he wasn't nearly as fast as Audrey.

She made it to Phoebe before Nash, grabbed the spilled beer off the floor, said something funny and had the entire table laughing. Then she wagged a finger at the cowboy and warned him to leave the new girl alone. Phoebe had enough to worry about.

The cowboy nodded, his face contrite under Audrey's chastising. "Sorry, Miss Phoebe. It won't happen again."

His buddies roared with laughter and clapped him on the back.

Phoebe and Audrey gathered all the empty bottles and returned to the bar with no further trouble.

"Not interested, huh?" Beckett stood beside Nash.

"You sure were up in a hurry. And I know it wasn't for another beer. The bar is in the other direction."

"Doesn't mean anything. After rescuing her on the side of the road, I feel responsible for her welfare."

"Yeah. And she isn't cute enough to make you jealous of the guy who pinched her."

Nash's brows descended. "It's sexual harassment."

"And he apologized," Beckett pointed out.

"Still, he bears watching."

"He?" Beckett asked with an arched eyebrow. "Or she?"

Nash had enough of his brother's taunts. Rather than stick around for more of their good-natured abuse, he pushed through the front door and out into the open night air. The moonless sky was no less bright with the blanket of stars shining down on the Texas landscape.

He breathed in and let go of the tension he hadn't been able to shuck since he'd met the fiery-haired temptress on the road to Hellfire. If he'd known then she'd be staying in Hellfire indefinitely, he might not have been so helpful. Oh, who was he kidding? An hour after he was supposed to have reported in for shift change, he'd dragged his ass into the sheriff's office. When he filled out his report, he'd found himself deleting half of the words he'd typed on the screen.

The sheriff and the county records didn't need to know the woman was young, and pretty with pale, moss green eyes. They sure as hell didn't need to know she bit her bottom lip whenever she was nervous and that the action made Nash want to kiss her every time she did it. When he'd finally made his way to the ranch, he'd had every intention of going for a long ride on his horse to clear the woman from his head.

The ride had to be postponed as he'd promised to go with his brothers to the Ugly Stick Saloon to celebrate Chance's birthday. If he could have gotten out of it, he would have. But today was his brother's birthday and they'd promised each other to pick up where their parents had left off after their untimely deaths. They were family, and family stuck together.

Except when they were pushing him toward a woman who had trouble written all over her pretty face.

Nash walked across the gravel parking lot, tempted to climb in his truck and head back to the ranch. He'd done his duty and drank a toast to his brother's birthday. They wouldn't begrudge him calling it a day, considering he'd been on duty since five o'clock that morning. But the farther away from the saloon he walked, the more it called to him to return.

Hell, the saloon wasn't what called to him to return. His protective instincts were on high-alert for the little redhead on her first day as a waitress. He couldn't ignore her or go home now that he knew she would be there all evening, surrounded by a bunch of rowdy cowboys, who would most likely drink themselves stupid and come on to every waitress in the bar— including Phoebe and Audrey.

Jackson would be there to help Audrey close up. He always was on rodeo nights. He loved his wife, the mother of his baby girl, and didn't want her to be manhandled by a drunken cowboy. Audrey was just as much of a temptation as the other waitresses with her strawberry blonde hair, short cutoffs and bright red cowboy boots. She'd made something out of the Ugly Stick Saloon and the bar was getting a reputation for the place to go when cowboys and travelers were anywhere near the tri-county area.

Resisting the urge to return to the saloon, knowing he couldn't keep his gaze off Phoebe, Nash walked around the building, staring out at the hayfields bathed in starlight. He loved the wide-open spaces and the fresh, clean country air.

After four combat tours before he'd turned twenty-seven, he was glad to be home. Two years of ranching later had barely taken the edge off his military duty. With more nervous energy than even he could stand, he'd signed on with the local sheriff's department. It was just another way to stay busy and continue the ingrained need to serve and protect the people of his country and community. Otherwise, the transition back to the civilian world would have been even harder, and he might have ended up like some of his buddies who couldn't seem to find their way home.

He had his family, the ranch and the open spaces where he could escape when he needed to. Lights shined on him from a vehicle turning around at the back of the building. Nash glanced to the side to make sure he wasn't in the way. As a deputy with the sheriff's department, he couldn't help but study the make and model and commit the license plate to memory.

Most of the vehicles in the parking lot were trucks or SUVs. The vehicle making the turn was a dark, four-door sedan, either navy blue or black. The windows were darkly tinted, disguising how many people were inside. And if that wasn't enough to make the hairs on the back of Nash's neck stand at attention, the vehicle moved slowly, as if the driver was looking for someone or something.

Nash stood near a tree, outside the glow of the pale yellow light on the back porch of the saloon. He doubted the sedan's driver had seen him, or he probably wouldn't be casing the joint or the other trucks and SUVs in the parking lot.

As the sedan rounded the side of the saloon aiming for the front, Nash followed the glowing brake lights.

The sedan performed the same routine, driving the length of the parking area, turning and driving just as slowly back. Finally, the driver pulled out onto the highway and sped off.

Armed with the license plate, Nash called in to Martha, the woman on night duty at dispatch.

A few moments later, she called back. "The vehicle belongs to a Frances Maynard, an eighty-year-old woman living in Fort Worth."

Which could explain why she was driving so slowly, but not why she was in the area to begin with —unless she was looking for her husband. In which case, the car should have been in his name as well. "And it wasn't reported stolen?"

"No. Why do you ask?"

"I saw it cruising around the Ugly Stick Saloon. You might have someone call Mrs. Maynard and ask her if she knows where her car is."

"This late at night?"

"If it was stolen, the sooner we know, the sooner we can recover it."

"Will do," Martha said and ended the call.

With that odd feeling still prickling the skin on the back of his neck, Nash rounded to the front door and entered the saloon, his gaze going automatically to the redhead serving drinks to his brothers.

Rider was smiling and talking to Phoebe, like he always did with the women. Normally, his flirting didn't bother Nash. Rider fancied himself a ladies' man. Only this time, it rubbed Nash the wrong way. Maybe his brothers were right, and he was jealous of any man flirting with Phoebe. So what? Didn't mean he wanted her for himself. He just didn't want anyone else to have her.

He cursed beneath his breath and marched across the wooden dance floor to the table he'd been sharing with Beckett, Kinsey, Chance and Rider. Audrey had come to sit with them, taking the seat Nash vacated.

When he arrived at the table, she hopped up.

"No need to leave." Nash genuinely enjoyed Audrey's company, her sharp mind and business sense when it came to running the Ugly Stick Saloon. She'd helped more than her share of what he called "stray" humans get back on their feet when they hit hard times. The woman had a big heart and an open door. If someone needed something, she was there to help.

"I have to get back to work," Audrey insisted. "I just wanted to wish Chance a happy birthday. Sit," she commanded. "Phoebe was about to take orders."

Nash sat in the chair, still warm from where Audrey had been. When he glanced up at Phoebe, her gaze met his. She drew her bottom lip between her teeth and worried it, before asking. "Can I get you anything?"

"Long neck, Bud Light," he said, his voice gruff, the urge to kiss that bottom lip stronger than ever before.

Phoebe nodded, spun on her heels and hurried away.

"Hey," Rider said, a frown denting his brow. "She didn't take my order."

"If you weren't so busy flirting, you might have told her," Beckett said.

"You snooze, you lose," Chance added with a smirk.

Rider shrugged. "That's okay. I need to move." He glanced around the saloon until his gaze landed on two women sitting at a table on the opposite side of the dance floor. Clapping his hands together, Rider grinned. "I'm seeing double tonight. Maybe I'll get twice as lucky."

"Aren't they a little young for you?" Beckett asked.

"As far as I know, they're single, live on their own and are over twenty-one." Shooting a frown at Beckett, he added, "I'm not that much older."

"Nine years is a big gap to a twenty-one-year-old woman," Chance agreed.

"Eight. I'm not thirty yet. And you're just jealous you didn't see them first." He tipped his head toward them. "Tell you what, I'll let you have one of them, while I dance with the other."

"Assuming they say yes." Chance stood. "You can have both. I prefer my women a little more seasoned."

Rider rested his hand on his brother's shoulder, his lips twisting. "That's right, you're in the over-thirty age group now. You like them a little slower so that you can catch them."

Chance punched Rider in the arm. "Keep it up, little brother. You're turning thirty in a couple of months."

"Yeah, but I'll be secure in the knowledge that you will always be older." Rubbing his shoulder, he made a beeline for the Banks twins, Hayley and Alexis.

Nash shook his head. He and Rider used to tease each other endlessly when they were teens. One year apart in age, they'd had the same friends in school and went to the same places. Since Nash had joined the army, he'd lost some of the ease of familiarity they'd shared as kids. Realizing he and Rider weren't as close as they once were made him sad. The war had changed Nash. Joking around like he had before deploying to the Middle East and Afghanistan wasn't as easy. He'd seen too much death. At times, he wished he could be that kid again, without a care, his mind still innocent of the atrocities humans suffered at the hands of terrorists.

"Sorry I took so long," a soft voice said.

A beer appeared on the table in front of him. While he'd been watching Rider and Chance spar verbally, Kinsey had dragged Beckett to the dance floor. Nash sat alone but for the redheaded waitress leaning over him. He inhaled, expecting the scent of honeysuckle, only it wasn't honeysuckle, instead she smelled kind of citrusy. Nash almost opened his mouth and said he wished she still smelled of honeysuckle.

Phoebe laid her tray on the table and slipped into the chair beside him, her bare knee touching his jean-clad leg.

In that moment, Nash wished his leg was as bare and touching hers, skin to skin.

She reached out and touched his arm. "Thank you for helping me today. I don't know what I would have done if you hadn't come along." She gave him a tremulous smile. "You were like a knight in shining armor, swooping me out of the mess I'd gotten myself into. Now, I have clothes, shoes, a place to stay and a job. All in less than twenty-four hours." Her smile widened, and she pulled a wad of cash out of her pocket. "And the bar patrons tipped me enough to pay for a tire."

He curled his fingers around hers and the cash. "You need to call the rental car company and have them pay for the repairs." The woman who hadn't had a cent to her name, probably didn't have food in her pantry, yet she was more concerned about fixing a tire to a vehicle that didn't belong to her. "They probably have insurance to cover tires and fender benders. You should keep your cash and buy a loaf of bread."

"Oh, I will," she said. "But I want to pay your brother first. I'd like to have it back as soon as possible." She pulled her hand away and toyed with the edge of the drink tray. "Umm, the rental is paid through next week. I hope I can figure out some kind of transportation by then. I'll get the rental car company to reimburse me later." Phoebe jumped to her feet and grabbed the tray. "I'd better get back to work. There are so many thirsty men in this place." She rushed away, glancing back with a worried expression, her bottom lip clamped firmly between her teeth.

For some reason, she seemed to be running scared about something.

Something didn't ring true with Phoebe Smith. As chatty as the woman was, she was holding back. Nash couldn't quite put his finger on what it was she wasn't telling him, but he was determined find out. Which, unfortunately, meant spending more time with the woman.

A dangerous prospect based on the way his arm tingled where she'd touched it and his leg ached to be naked against hers. Yeah, spending time with her could only be a mistake. But his curiosity was piqued and, like a dog with a bone, he couldn't let go. Not yet.

CHAPTER 6

PHOEBE HURRIED AWAY FROM NASH, rubbing her arm. When she'd touched Nash, an electrical current had tingled in her fingers and run up her arm. It spread through her chest and downward, pooling at the base of her belly. Why? He was a stranger. She'd never felt that way about her fiancé. The hot, aching, needy tension swelled inside her.

Why this man?

As the band ended its set, a loud crash jerked Phoebe out of her sensual stupor. She rushed forward, eager to help clean up whatever mess resulted from the accident.

Audrey yelped and hopped up to sit on the bar.

The patrons of the saloon grew silent, all gazes turned toward Audrey.

Phoebe hurried around the corner of the bar to find a trail of broken glass and spilled whiskey.

Worse, Audrey bled from a large gash in her knee. "Oh, Audrey, you're bleeding." Phoebe grabbed a bar towel from a drawer and applied pressure to the cut. She eased it away and examined the wound. It looked ugly, but didn't scare Phoebe. Her love of horses had given her a healthy respect for keeping her cool around scratches, cuts and bruises. "Looks pretty deep. You might need stitches."

"Well, damn." Audrey stared down at her leg. "I don't have time for stitches." She waved a hand toward the swarms of cowboys crowding the bar to capacity. "We can't afford to lose another waitress tonight."

Jackson appeared from the storeroom, carrying a case of whiskey. "What happened?" He nearly tossed the case on the ground and hurried forward, picking his way across the glass-strewn floor.

"I broke a whiskey bottle, slipped in the whiskey and landed on my knee." Audrey sighed. "Do you think you can put a bandage on it so I can finish out the night?"

Nash leaned over the bar. "Bring her over to the table and let Chance have a look. He's the trained EMT."

Alerted to the problem, Chance pushed his way through the crowded room.

Jackson carried Audrey over to set her on a nearby table.

Chance examined the wound.

Audrey's assistant manager, Charli Sutton, emerged from the storeroom, carrying the first aid kit, and laid it on the table beside Audrey.

Phoebe stepped out of the way and helped Libby clean up the broken glass and whiskey.

Chance applied a pressure bandage to the gash on Audrey's leg, and then glanced at Jackson. "She's bleeding through the bandage. She really needs to see a doctor and have it stitched. I can call for an ambulance, or you can take her to the emergency room yourself."

"Oh, please, I'm not going to die. Jackson can take me to the ER." Audrey nodded to Libby. "Do you mind closing the saloon tonight?"

Charli shook her head. "The woman's bleeding, and she still can't let go of this place." The bartender waved her hand. "Get out of here before you bleed to death. We've got this covered, don't we, Phoebe?"

Phoebe straightened with a dustpan full of glass shards. "Please. Go to the doctor. Your health is more important. Like Charli said, we can handle it."

"But we've got so many customers," Audrey protested.

Charli climbed up on the bar and motioned for Lacey, one of the other waitresses working that night, to pull the plug on the jukebox.

As the room grew quiet and all heads turned toward Charli, she tossed her curly blond hair over her shoulder and then stood with her fists on her hips. "Do y'all promise to behave while Audrey goes to the hospital?"

"Hell yeah!" rose a shout from every man and woman in the saloon.

Charli turned to Audrey, "There you have it. Now go. I'll open tomorrow, so don't you worry."

"Come on." Jackson scooped Audrey into his arms. "Can't have the mother of my baby girl bleeding out in a bar." He winked and carried her through the back room to the rear exit.

Phoebe watched until they disappeared and then turned to Libby. "Okay. What now?"

Charli grinned. "Get to work covering her tables. Between me, Libby, you and Lacey, we can handle it. Thanks for showing up when you did."

While Libby filled her order, Phoebe ran to another table, returned with their order, slapped it on the bar and took the full tray to distribute the drinks. For the next two hours, she repeated the process, doing her best to keep the thirsty cowboys satisfied.

Throughout the evening, Nash sat at a table with his brothers until, one by one, they left to go home. Each time another Grayson rose, Phoebe's gaze shifted to Nash, and she wondered if he would leave with them. But he hadn't.

The crowd swelled near midnight and stayed full and rowdy until after one-thirty when the men finally clamped their hats on their heads and left to rest up for another day at the rodeo.

Her back and feet aching, Phoebe worked on, cleaning up the empty bottles, mugs and shot glasses. After the last cowboy left, Phoebe helped Charli and Lacey stack the chairs on the tables. Mops in hand, they cleaned up the spilled beer, whiskey and sodas from the floor.

Tired to the bone, she rinsed out her mop and hung it to dry outside off the back porch. Despite her exhaustion, she couldn't help but feel better about her situation. Her pockets were full of bills from all the tips she'd earned.

Charli hung her mop beside Phoebe's. "For a newbie, you did good. Thanks for sticking it out. Rodeo week can be a killer."

"I'm glad I could help." She rubbed her hands on her jean cutoffs and straightened her back. "I hope Audrey will be okay."

"Jackson called an hour ago. After ten stitches and a painkiller, Audrey is sleeping. He has baby duty through the night." Charli smiled. "I've never seen a grown man so over the moon about a little girl as he is. Emma is one lucky baby."

"Audrey and Jackson seem to love each other a great deal."

"If you work here long enough, you're bound to run across them getting it on in the storeroom. Just fair warning." Charli winked. "And they don't mind if you watch."

Phoebe's eyes widened. "Really?"

"Their love is true and they aren't afraid to show it." Charli pushed her long blond hair back behind her ear. "You better get home and grab some sleep. If you're available tomorrow, we could sure use your help."

"I can work," Phoebe said and then frowned. "Only thing is I might not have a way to get here."

Charli tapped her chin with the tip of her finger. "Where are you staying?"

"In Hellfire. I'm renting a garage apartment from a woman named Lola."

"Let me work on the logistics. If I can't find someone coming out from Hellfire, I'll swing by myself. We can't manage this rodeo crowd without your help."

Phoebe's chest filled with warmth at the praise. Never having held a job, she didn't know how good working felt. Putting in a hard day's effort, gave her a greater appreciation for the staff that made her family home sparkle.

"Charli, I could use a hand in here," Libby called out.

The assistant manager turned to go back into the saloon before Phoebe had a chance to tell her Audrey was supposed to be her ride home. She'd have to catch her before she left. But for that moment, Phoebe stared out at the starlit Texas night.

A shadow detached itself from the only tree behind the building and a man wearing a cowboy hat walked toward her.

A flash of caution made Phoebe take a step backward and reach for the doorknob. She twisted the handle, without taking her gaze off the man whose face she couldn't make out in the shadow from the hat's rim. "Who's there?" she asked, her fingers turning the knob behind her back. It didn't turn. The door had closed and locked automatically.

Her pulse kicked up a notch, slamming blood through her veins in double-time.

"It's okay," he said. "It's me, Nash Grayson."

She let go of the breath she'd drawn in, and laughed shakily. "Don't scare me like that."

Deputy Grayson nodded toward the door behind her. "It locked, didn't it?"

Phoebe grimaced. "Yeah. I'll have to go around the front to get in." She tilted her head to the side. "I thought you'd left a long time ago."

"I left when the saloon closed, but sat in my truck. Figured you might need a ride back to Hellfire. Most of the waitresses who work here live in or near Temptation. It's the opposite direction from where you need to go."

She smiled. "Thanks. Jackson gave me a ride here and Audrey was going to take me home, but from the sound of it, I need to find alternate transportation. I don't like being a burden on anyone."

"Rider should be able to get a tire on that rental car by tomorrow, if you give him the go ahead."

She pulled the wad of cash from her pocket and held it up. "Not bad, for my first night." Phoebe pushed the money back into her pocket and descended the steps to the ground. "I'll check with Charli and Libby. If they don't need me anymore, I'm ready to leave."

Deputy Grayson nodded and accompanied her around the side of the saloon. The parking lot was empty except for the two vehicles in the back and a truck Phoebe assumed belonged to the deputy.

Phoebe stopped at the front door and turned to face Nash. "You know, just because you rescued me from the side of the road today, doesn't mean you're responsible for me."

His brows rose and his lips quirked upward on the corners. "Do you want me to leave you to walk back to Hellfire?"

The thought of running into the two men from earlier sent a chill slithering across the back of her neck. But she shook her head. "No, I don't want you to leave me to walk. I didn't want to ask Libby or Charli for a ride, because I know they live toward Temptation, and they're as tired as I am."

"Then it's settled." He opened the door and held it. "I'm giving you a ride home. Not out of a sense of responsibility, but because I'm headed that direction anyway."

"Oh. Okay." She found Charli and Libby in the storeroom. "Need me to stick around?"

"We're done here." Charli gathered empty boxes in her arms and straightened. "See you tomorrow, then?"

If she wasn't in jail for murder. "You bet." She turned to find Deputy Grayson behind her. How ironic to have him taking her back to Hellfire when he might be the one to haul her off to jail when someone stumbled on the body in the trunk of her rental car.

Too tired to care and thinking the bed in the jail house sounded like heaven, Phoebe smiled. "I'm ready." For whatever is thrown my way. After the day she'd had, her luck couldn't get worse. And she still had to find a way to get Ryan's body out of the trunk before someone discovered it.

As THEY LEFT THE SALOON, Nash hooked his hand through Phoebe's elbow and steered her toward his truck, the only vehicle left in the front parking area. "You never said where you're from."

"No, I didn't," she responded.

Shaking off the bolt of electricity inspired by touching Phoebe, Nash laughed. "I take it you still aren't going to tell me."

"No. And if you're going to question me all the way back to Hellfire, I'll have to pass on the ride." She pulled free of his grip and stepped away from truck. "Charli could give me a ride back."

Nash held up a hand. "Okay, okay. I promise not to grill you." He opened the passenger door and held it. "We don't even have to talk, if you don't want to. That's fine by me."

Her brows dipped, and she studied him for a moment before finally climbing into the cab. "Thank you for not pushing it. And for the ride."

"You're welcome." He closed the door and shook his head as he rounded the front of the vehicle and climbed in. As he pulled out onto the highway, he glanced her way.

Phoebe stared out the window, her bottom lip snagged between her teeth.

"You don't have to worry. I promise not to grill you," he said, shifting his focus to the road ahead. He fought to keep from asking her all the questions running through his mind. The woman was an enigma. What made her run away on the day of her wedding? Did her fiancé have an affair with one of her bridesmaids? Or was he abusive?

Nash's fingers curled tightly around the steering wheel.

"Have you lived all your life in Hellfire?"

Her voice was soft, slipping across him like a

caress. Nash nodded. "All except my time in college and the military."

She shot a glance his way. "You were in the military?"

He nodded. "Six years. I joined straight out of college."

"Why?"

His chin rose automatically. "I consider living in this country to be a privilege, not a right. I wanted to give back for all I've been given." Nash could feel Phoebe's stare burning into him.

"Did you fight in the war?"

Jaw tightening, he nodded. Fought, killed and watched his troops and friends die. At the ripe old age of twenty-seven, he'd lived a lifetime.

"I don't think I've ever actually met someone who has served." She shook her head, a sad smile lifting the corners of her lips. Her hand touched his arm. "Thank you for your service."

He glanced down at the slim fingers on his arm and then returned his attention to the road.

"Was it hard?" She let her hand drop to her lap. "Being in the military and away from your family, that is."

He shook his head. "When you're in a unit, your peers are your family. You'd fight and die for them." Although, the hard part was watching them die.

"You must have loved them."

His eyes stung. Nash had pushed those memories

as far to the back of his mind as he could since he'd left the army. His time in Afghanistan seemed like another life. He'd been a different person than the one he was now. Images flashed through his memories of the men with whom he'd served—many of whom died in the final battle that ended his career and gave him a banged-up knee.

"Why did you leave the military?"

"So it's okay for you to ask me questions, but I can't ask you any?" he bit out. "I left because they kicked me out. Otherwise, I'd still be over in some hellhole, fighting for my life and the lives of my men."

"Kicked you out?" she persisted.

"Medically retired, due to an injury." Thankfully, they weren't far from Hellfire. In a few short minutes, he'd drop her off, and he wouldn't have to answer any more of her questions.

A long pause stretched between them and Nash thought Phoebe had given up on her interrogation.

"You lost some friends, didn't you?"

He slammed a palm against the steering wheel, feeling as though she'd ripped open a wound in his heart. "Yes, damn it!" He'd lost too many.

Her soft, "I'm sorry," spread over him like warm butter, melting into his pores, slowly calming him. His grip on the steering wheel loosened and he eased up on the accelerator.

Phoebe glanced his way again. "You get around pretty well."

His knee twinged, the familiar burning sensation flaring whenever he thought about it. Since they'd replaced the kneecap, the joint worked pretty well. But it would never be the same as before he'd been hit. The muscles and tendons were still getting used to the replacement. He'd been lucky enough to live to get that new knee. So many of his men hadn't had the choice. "Yeah, well not good enough for the army." If he could have gone back to fight, he would have. If for nothing else than to exact revenge on those who'd ambushed him and his troops.

"Really, I'm sorry for your loss." Phoebe faced forward again.

For a long moment, silence reigned.

Memories spun in Nash's head, happy times joking with his men, heartbreaking times when he'd knelt beside a soldier whose life ebbed away with injuries so horrific he had no hope of recovery. "Tell my wife I love her," were his last words. Nash's heart clenched and his vision blurred. What must it have felt like to know you were dying, leaving the woman you loved to face the world without you?

"Was it hard starting over once you got back to Texas?" Phoebe asked, her voice little more than a whisper, her gaze on him.

"I've been home for almost two years, and I'm still not sure how I fit in, or if I ever will." He turned into Lola's driveway, thankful they'd arrived and that Phoebe's line of questioning, and all the thoughts and feelings it resurrected, would end. "I can give you a lift to the Ugly Stick Saloon tomorrow evening, if you like." God, why had he opened his big mouth? But now that he'd said it, he couldn't take back the offer.

She smiled. "Thank you. But I hope to have the rental car back by then. I can use it while looking for alternate transportation."

"The offer is open. All you have to do is call." He reached for the door handle. Her hand on his arm stopped him.

"I can get out by myself." Phoebe leaned over and pressed her lips to his cheek. "I, for one, am glad you're back from the war. If you hadn't come along when you did, I don't know what I would have done. Thanks again."

The softness of her lips on his face muddled his brain. Before Nash could think to move, Phoebe was out of the truck and halfway to the garage apartment.

She turned and gave him a little wave and then ran up the stairs, unlocked the door and disappeared inside.

Nash sat for a long moment, staring at the empty stairs as lights blinked on inside Phoebe's apartment. He touched his cheek where her lips had been, the residual warmth spreading from that point throughout his body and downward, his groin tightening.

Hell. He'd opened up more with her than with his

own brothers. With them, he put on the tough-guy face and kept his thoughts about his time in the military to himself. His brothers had their own lives. Chance was a fireman, racing into burning buildings on a daily basis. Beckett ran the ranch, facing raging bulls and angry, grass fires, bucking horses and rattlesnakes as part of his everyday life. Rider, well... Rider had his own business towing and fixing vehicles. They had dangerous jobs and big responsibilities. But how could any of them relate to what Nash had done in the military? He'd witnessed men being blown apart, and held his buddy in his arms as he took his last breath. Horrors like that weren't things a man forgot. Ever.

Throwing the shift lever into Reverse, Nash backed out of Lola's driveway and onto the street. What was it about Phoebe that made him stay at the bar until her shift ended? His brothers left around midnight. Nash had stayed until 2:00 a.m.

Whatever it was, he didn't need it. Phoebe and her sad green eyes and auburn hair didn't need another man in her life messing it up. Her situation was hard enough starting over with nothing but the clothes she'd gotten from a thrift shop. God, but she was determined, refusing to go crawling back home.

As he drove out of Hellfire, he spotted the dark sedan parked in front of the only motel in town, an old motor lodge built in the 1950s.

They'd probably been driving slowly through

town earlier, hoping to find a better alternative. Unfortunately, the motor lodge was the only game in town. They would have had to go to Temptation for something better. Temptation had a bed and breakfast. Both towns were too small to justify a large chain hotel.

His thoughts shifted back to Phoebe and he raised his hand to his cheek. Nash drove home. His head spun and his cheek burned with Phoebe's kiss and worst of all, he faced a day off. He hoped like hell Beckett had a list of chores for him to do. Since returning to the civilian world, having nothing to do meant having too much time to think about the past.

Maybe he'd head back to Hellfire early the next day and see what Phoebe was up to. The woman and her secrets revved Nash's interest more than he wanted to admit. Perhaps, after he discovered what she was hiding, the mystery would disappear and his interest would wane. They could all get back to a normal world and move on with their lives.

CHAPTER 7

PHOEBE WAITED several minutes inside her apartment, praying Nash would leave soon. What he'd shared had touched her so deeply, she could barely swallow past the lump in her throat. The things he'd endured as a soldier in the war were far worse than anything she'd had to go through. How did you compare a broken fingernail to losing men you care about because of bombs and gunfire?

More exhausted than she'd ever been in her life, Phoebe stared at the little bed with the clean sheets. She almost gave in and fell onto the mattress, fully clothed. She could have been asleep in seconds, but for the little matter of her dead fiancé in the trunk of the rental car.

With a sigh, she peered through the mini-blinds.

Nash's truck was gone. The only vehicle left was Lola's bright red 1967 Ford Mustang. The lights were off in the main house, as were the lights in the neighboring houses.

Phoebe grabbed an old steak knife from the kitchenette and flipped the switch next to the door, plunging herself into darkness. Giving herself a minute for her eyesight to adjust, she waited, hand on the doorknob. Then she turned it and hurried out of the apartment and down the stairs. Moving through the alley behind the house, she clung to the shadows and half-jogged, paralleling Main Street until she came to the road where Rider Grayson's auto repair shop stood.

She crossed Main Street and slipped to the back of the shop. With the knife in her hand, she slid it into the doorknob key hole and turned. Nothing. The movies made it look so easy. How did they do it? She tried slipping the knife into the doorjamb to jiggle the locking mechanism. The door was a heavy metal one, as was the jamb. She bent the knife trying.

Finally, Phoebe straightened and glanced around, gooseflesh rising on her arms. If she couldn't get in through the door, what about a window? The windows were those old warehouse style with multiple little panes on one major assembly. Phoebe grabbed several wooden pallets and stacked them beneath one of the windows then climbed onto the unsteady pile.

There in the middle of the shop was the rental car. Fortunately, the trunk was still closed. Unfortunately, the vehicle was up on a lift. To get into the building would be hard enough. Accessing the trunk while it was several feet off the ground would be nearly impossible.

Disappointed and too tired to care, Phoebe eased to the edge of the pile of pallets and started to slip off. The stack shifted, several of the pallets sliding off the top, taking her with it, making a loud cracking sound as wooden slats snapped.

A dog in a yard behind the shop barked, another joined, and soon lights lit up back porches and dog owners yelled at the barking dogs.

Heart pounding double-time, Phoebe rolled off the pallets, jumped to her feet and beat a hasty retreat back to the garage apartment. First thing in the morning, she'd run by the shop and wait for Rider to change the tire.

If the sheriff didn't show up first, slap cuffs on her wrists and haul her off to jail.

Yeah, she'd be sleeping like a baby tonight.

Not.

Stripping out of the clothes she'd worn to work, she showered and fell into the twin bed and stared up at the ceiling, going through all that had happened that day. Nowhere in her memories could she come up with a reason why someone would want to kill Ryan, or an image of anyone who might have done the dirty deed.

His best man had been beside himself with worry

over Ryan's disappearance. Who else could have done it?

She'd been so busy getting ready and wondering if she'd made a huge mistake, she hadn't really seen anyone or had a thought to spare of her fiancé, other than knowing he wasn't the man for her.

As she rolled the memory movie through her mind, she came to the part where Deputy Grayson swooped in like a knight in shining armor and rescued her from the fencepost. From that point on, he'd been there to help her. Even taking her to a thrift shop to find clothes. Why?

Part of her wanted him to stay away until she resolved what to do with her fiancé's body. Hell, if she was smart, she would confess her crime of stealing the convertible to the authorities and face the consequences. Hiding her part in the whole fiasco only made her look even guiltier of killing Ryan.

If she relinquished the body, she would have to reveal her true identity. Her father would bail her out as usual, and she'd be forced to go back to her life as the daughter of a wealthy man. He might even choose her next husband.

Her father would consider her work at the Ugly Stick Saloon to be beneath the daughter of Jonathon Sinclair, but it had felt good. Well, her back and feet did ache, but in a good way. Like she'd earned the sore muscles rather than paid for a physical trainer to deliver the pain.

After spending time with Nash and getting a feeling of his anguish from his time in the military, Phoebe realized her life had been meaningless. While men fought and died for their country, she'd been more concerned about what shoes to wear with the latest outfit she'd purchased. Some of those outfits had cost more than what a soldier brought home in his paycheck in a month. Maybe two or three.

Shame washed over her. Maybe she wouldn't join the military, but she could change for the better and become a contributing member of society, rather than being a society debutante. Going back to her old life with her family was not an option.

Phoebe yawned and stretched. The hard work weighed on her body and mind. Before she knew it, she'd slipped into a deep sleep, strangely empty of the nightmares she'd expected.

She didn't wake until someone pounded on the door.

Light streamed into the little apartment around the edges of the closed blinds.

Phoebe blinked and rubbed her eyes, wondering what had pulled her out of the depths of her sleep. She rolled over and nearly fell out of the tiny bed. More pounding on the door made her sit up with a start.

"Phoebe!" Lola's voice sounded from outside.

"Coming." She leaped to her feet, tugged down the oversized T-shirt she'd worn to bed the night before and hurried the few short steps to open the door.

"Oh, good. You're up." Lola pushed her hair back from her made-up face. "I thought I'd have to let myself in to wake you."

"What's wrong?" Phoebe asked, crossing her arms over her middle.

"Just got a call from the sheriff's office." She drew in a deep breath and paused.

Her heart slipping into the bottom of her belly, Phoebe waited for what was coming next. They had to have found the body in the trunk. The sheriff would be there momentarily to arrest her. With an apology poised on her lips, Phoebe opened her mouth to beg forgiveness for getting Lola involved with a murder suspect.

Lola's eyes gleamed. "Rider Grayson's auto shop was broken into last night. The rental car he was working on for you was stolen."

"WHAT DO YOU MEAN, your shop was broken into?" Nash balanced the telephone between his cheek and shoulder as he dragged on his jeans and zipped. He sat on the side of his bed and pulled on his cowboy boots.

"Someone broke a window and entered my shop. They lowered the rental car on the lift, opened the overhead door and drove away without anyone noticing. The sheriff thinks it must have happened between 3:00 and 4:00 a.m. this morning." Rider paused. "Funny thing is they didn't take anything but the car. The cash box was intact where I'd left it in the office."

"Has anyone checked on Miss Smith?"

"The sheriff was going to notify her."

"I'll be in town in a few minutes."

"It's your day off," Rider said. "Let others handle it."

"I want to make sure Phoebe is all right." Whoever broke into the shop for the rental car might also have gone after the woman. Unless the woman was responsible for the break-in. In which case, she might have left town. To make matters worse, he'd had some pretty lusty thoughts about a potential criminal.

"I'm sure the sheriff would let you know if she wasn't."

Not in the mood to argue, Nash said, "I'll see you in a few." He ended the call and finished dressing. He hadn't wanted to face an empty day. Well now, he wouldn't have to. Finding a missing vehicle would keep him busy.

And checking in on Phoebe Smith would be purely part of the job. Purely.

Deep inside, he couldn't ignore the hope Phoebe wasn't the one who'd entered the shop and taken the vehicle. Now that he'd met her, Nash didn't want her to leave town so soon. He still had so many unanswered questions. But that wasn't all. He found himself drawn to the woman who had insisted on starting over in a strange town. What had she run away from? What did she hope to gain by moving to the small community of Hellfire?

The first question he intended to answer was, had Phoebe left Hellfire in the rental car?

Tugging a T-shirt over his head, he grabbed his belt and ran for the door.

Beckett stepped out of the kitchen, a coffee cup in hand. "Where are you going?"

"Town."

"I thought you might help me repair the fence in the northeast pasture today."

"Rain check. I have something I need to check on in town." Not something, but someone.

"I guess Kinsey can help. She's better looking, anyway."

Kinsey stepped up beside him. "And I can swing a hammer." She slipped an arm around Beckett's waist and leaned against him.

Nash retrieved his cowboy hat from a hook on the wall and left the house. He was halfway to town when his cell phone rang in the cup holder. He checked the number and recognized it as Lola's. His pulse hammering, he clicked the talk button. "Lola. Tell me Phoebe's all right."

"This is Phoebe."

Her warm voice filled his ear and spread heat throughout his body. He sighed.

"I guess you've heard," she said.

"I have," he responded. "I'm glad you're still in town."

"Why would I leave?" She paused. "Oh, wait. You thought I might have been the one to break into your brother's shop. Fair enough. I haven't given you much to go on. But we need to talk."

"I'll be there in fifteen minutes."

"Good." She sighed. "Just keep in mind, I've never been in trouble with the law before. And I didn't ask for it."

The connection ended before he could question her more. What did she mean by she'd never been in trouble with the law before? Was she now?

A thousand questions bubbled up in his mind. He pressed harder on the accelerator, impatient with the amount of time it took to get from the ranch to town. By the time he pulled into Lola's driveway, he'd broken a few of the speed limits he was sworn to uphold as a man of the law.

Lola stood near her Mustang with a crooked smile on her face. "Where's the fire, cowboy?" She tipped her head toward the garage apartment. "Wish it was me you were in a hurry to see. Phoebe's in her apartment. Nothing like a little excitement to stir up things in Hellfire, huh?"

"Thanks for letting her use your phone," Nash said as he passed Lola and loped the rest of the way across the drive. He took the stairs two at a time and entered through the open doorway.

Phoebe stood with her back leaning against the tiny kitchenette counter, a cup of tea in her hands. The liquid sloshed over the sides because her hands shook so badly.

For a long moment, Nash stared. Her cheeks were pale, her green eyes dark, surrounded by shadows. As he crossed the room, her gaze sought his and her bottom lip trembled like her hands. She caught it between her teeth and her eyes filled.

Nash did the only thing he could. He took the cup from her, set it on the counter and then pulled her into his arms.

She rested her cheek against his chest, her fingers curling into his T-shirt. "I don't know how this all happened or why." A shiver shook her body, despite the heat already building outside.

"Tell me about it," he encouraged.

"I was supposed to get married yesterday."

"Already got that part."

She turned her face into his shirt and pressed her forehead to his chest, not looking up as the story spilled out. "The ceremony was about to begin when I realized I didn't love him. I almost married a man my father picked for me. Not one I loved." She waved a hand and then clutched his shirt again. "I don't know how I let the wedding plans go that far. Stupid, I guess. Gullible *and* stupid. I was about to go to him and tell him I couldn't marry him when the best man showed up and said they couldn't find the groom." She laughed.

The mirthless sound made Nash's heart contract. He stroked her curly auburn hair, wondering how any man could walk away from this woman. "He must have been a fool."

"I thought he'd jilted me. The irony wasn't lost on me, but I was angry. With myself. With my father. With Ryan. I looked for him. When I realized he wasn't in the church, I went outside, thinking he might be in the garden. He wasn't. And there it was. The convertible he should have been driving away from the church with me inside."

She leaned back and stared up at him, a film of tears making her eyes shine brightly. "For the first time in my life, I did what I wanted to do. Not what my father or mother wanted me to do. I got into that car and drove away from the church, from my life and from everything I knew. I was tired of being something I wasn't. Someone I didn't know or care to be." She smiled as the first tear trailed down her cheek.

Nash reached up to brush it away with his thumb, then he leaned forward and kissed her cheek.

"I didn't want to go back to live under my father's thumb, or marry a man of his choosing. I wanted to be independent. Live life as I saw fit." She threw her hands in the air, turned away and paced the three steps needed to cross the length of the available floor space. "Then the flat tire, the wreck and the body in the trunk. I got scared. I didn't know what to do. I thought I would be accused of murder." As her words poured out in a jumble, she raked a hand through her hair and spun toward him, her eyes wide. "I don't want to go to jail. I didn't do anything wrong. But I actually did because I didn't tell anyone." She extended her arms, her wrists held together. "You might as well arrest me. I'm sure I broke some law. But I didn't kill my fiancé."

Nash raised his hands. "Whoa! Slow down there. What are you talking about? Why would I arrest you?" Once again, he gathered her in his arms, hoping to comfort her. Then his mind picked two words out of her jumbled diatribe, and he froze. Slowly, he pushed her to arm's length, his brows lowered. "Wait. What body are you talking about? What murder?"

She stood staring, her entire body trembling now. "I told you. Ryan was in that trunk. My fiancé. He was dead."

CHAPTER 8

AFTER AN HOUR and a half in the sheriff's office, and a painfully thorough interrogation by the sheriff himself, Phoebe asked, "Now what? Am I going to jail?"

The sheriff shrugged. "We don't have a body. A missing persons report has been filed on Bratton, but there was a break-in and a car stolen. Again, we don't have the evidence of the missing car, so I can't really arrest you."

Phoebe let go of the breath she'd been holding. "And my family? Will they be notified?"

"Only if you want me to let them know," the sheriff said. "You're a grown woman. You don't have to tell your family anything."

"No. I'd rather they didn't learn where I am until I'm good and ready to let them know myself. Will any of my testimony be shared containing my name?"

"No, ma'am. Again, you haven't been arrested, so you won't go on the docket or be shared across departments." He pushed back his chair and stood. "Miss Sinclair, you're free to go."

Phoebe glanced around, looking for Nash. The deputy had excused him shortly after Phoebe had started relating her story. He hadn't returned, nor had she left the sheriff's office the entire time.

"Do you want me to have one of the deputies drive you home, Miss Sinclair?"

She shook her head, hoping Nash hadn't left the building. "No, it isn't too far to walk."

"I'm concerned about what you said about the two men who chased you last night." The sheriff tipped his head, a frown deepening the lines across his forehead. "I guess you'll be okay in broad daylight. But you should keep your night forays to a minimum, or go out with a friend. No use tempting fate or the bad guys."

Since she had a job working nights, staying inside at night was impossible. She had to get to and from work. Stiffening her spine, Phoebe held out her hand. "Thank you, Sheriff Olson. I'll be careful."

"You might consider letting your folks know you're okay." His big hand enveloped hers in a reassuring grip. "I keep thinking my daughter is about your age. I'd want to know she was safe."

"I'll think about it," she said. "My father is very overbearing. I'd like to put off the confrontation a

ELLE JAMES

little longer." At least until she was firmly on her own two feet and established in Hellfire. Then she'd let her father know she was okay and not coming home anytime soon.

She stepped out of the sheriff's office, and Nash hooked her elbow and hustled her toward the exit. "You could have told me you were the daughter of Jonathon Sinclair, the richest man in Texas."

Anger rolled off him like puffs of steam. Pulling her arm free of his grip, Phoebe lifted her chin and marched on her own toward the door. "I am not my father. I'm just Phoebe."

"Well, Just Phoebe, your father has a statewide manhunt out for you, with a ten-thousand-dollar reward attached." He pushed through the door and held it for her.

"So?" She stopped and faced him, crossing both arms over her chest. "Are you turning me in and collecting?"

"Hell, no." Again, he gripped her arm and led her out into the parking lot. "I'm driving you back to your garage apartment and then going home. Today's my day off."

Irritation prickled her skin, and she stopped short of his truck. "Go home, Deputy Grayson. You aren't responsible for me. I can get back to my apartment on my own."

Scowling, he opened the passenger door of his truck and held it. "Get in."

"I've had enough of taking orders from the men in my life. Screw you!" She stepped around him and the truck, and marched across the parking lot.

"You're going the wrong way," he yelled.

Without looking in his direction, she turned and headed the other direction.

A chuckle sounded behind her. "Still going the wrong way." He caught up to her and gripped her arms. "I'm sorry. I don't like being lied to, so sue me."

For a long moment, she held her shoulders back and her chin up. Then she released the tension that had built inside since Lola woke her with the news that morning. "Deputy Grayson—"

"Nash," he corrected.

"Nash." She drew in a breath and let it out. "Despite the fact that I lied to you, I don't like lying, and I don't make a habit of it."

The anger leached from his face, and he released her. "Then why did you do it?"

Phoebe stared into his blue eyes. "What would you do if you ran away from a wedding in a car that didn't belong to you and discovered a body in the trunk about the time a sheriff's deputy rolled up behind you?" She flung her hand in the air, and assumed a high-pitched, sarcastic tone. "Hi, I'm a rich man's daughter with a dead man in my trunk. Could you help me get him out so I can be on my merry way?"

For a long moment, Nash stared into her face.

First one side of his mouth twitched upward, then the other. A moment later, he laughed so hard, he held onto his belly and bent double.

Phoebe had to admit the man was even hotter when he smiled. This was the first time she'd seen him laugh, much less smile. "You should laugh more often."

"And you should stop attracting trouble like bees to honey." He straightened and wiped the tears from his eyes. "Sweetheart, I can't imagine you killing a man."

Her heart flipped at the endearment, and her lips twitched. "I can't even kill a spider. How would I kill a man?" Her gaze slipped lower to the mouth that had a moment before been smiling. Now it wasn't. When his lips weren't pressed into the usual tight line, they were full and temptingly kissable. Phoebe swayed toward him, pressing a hand to his chest. "I need to get back to the apartment. I promised to clean Lola's house as payment for rent."

This time when Nash held open the door to his truck, Phoebe didn't argue. She brushed past him, her hip touching his, sending a shock of heat through her, reminding her he was way too sexy when he smiled, or laughed, or hell, if he just stood there with his broad shoulders and incredibly blue eyes.

Now was not the time to get involved. Especially with a man of the law. She forced herself to look out the side window instead of sneaking peeks at him. He could be the one to arrest her when the authorities finally found Ryan's body, and didn't find the men who'd killed him. Getting involved with her could cause Nash to lose his job. He didn't deserve to inherit her troubles by falling for her. Not that he would. But she sure felt the attraction and, given other circumstances, she might even fall for a guy like Nash Grayson.

They pulled into Lola's driveway, then Nash got out and opened her door for her. When she went to slide down from her seat, he grabbed her around the waist and lifted, setting her gently on the ground.

"So, you're cleaning Lola's house?" he said.

She nodded. "That's the plan."

His brows arched. "As a rich man's daughter, have you *ever* cleaned a house?"

Stiffening, Phoebe tilted her chin upward. "Not actually. But how hard could it be?"

"You have my number. Call if you have questions." He winked.

She was left standing in the driveway, thinking he was arrogant and a know-it-all. House cleaning wasn't rocket science. She could handle it.

An hour later, standing in an ever-growing blob of suds, she hated eating her words, and she loathed even more calling Nash for help. But if she didn't do something soon, the entire house might be buried in the seething, frothing mess emanating from the washing machine. She dove for the phone and dialed

Nash's number. "I cry uncle. Is there any possibility you're still in town, and could come over and tell me how to stop Lola's house from being consumed by bubbles?"

Laughter met her ear, and she was tempted to slam the phone onto the cradle, but she couldn't hang up when Nash was the only person she knew besides Lola. If she wanted to save Lola's house, she had to put up with Nash laughing at her.

Once he got past the initial bark of laughter, Nash said, "I'll be right there."

True to his word, he showed up fifteen minutes later and walked into the kitchen where the suds had completely covered the tile flooring. He followed the flow to the source, the older model washing machine. "What soap did you use in the washer?" he asked as he leaned over the machine and switched it off.

"The blue liquid I found under the kitchen sink that said detergent." She left him with the foaming machine and returned with a bottle of blue liquid.

"Honey, that's dishwashing detergent, not laundry detergent."

Heat swirled low in her belly when he called her *honey*. "What's the difference?"

He nodded toward the flood of bubbles. "The difference is how sudsy it gets. Laundry detergent is low-suds. Get me a plastic cup and a bucket. We have to get the water with the soap in it out of the washer tub, and then run the rinse cycle several times to get the soap out of the clothes."

Forty-five minutes later, the clothes were rinsed and in the dryer, and the bubbles had been mopped up, making the floor sparkling clean.

Phoebe's stomach rumbled, and she pressed a hand to it.

Nash smiled. "Hungry?"

For a moment she couldn't think past the way his mouth curved upward and his blue eyes shone. Then her belly sounded off again. Phoebe laughed. "I guess I am. With everything that's happened this morning, I suppose I forgot to eat."

He grabbed her hand. "Come on. Bob's Diner has the best burgers in town."

"No." She pulled back. "I need to go to the store and stock up on groceries. I can't spend all my money on a burger. I have to make my tip-money last all week."

"I'm buying."

She shook her head. "You've already done too much for me by taking me to work and back."

"Then consider having lunch with me returning the favor. I don't like to eat alone."

Phoebe chewed on her bottom lip. When her stomach protested yet again, she sighed. "Okay. But I'll pay for my own."

Nash didn't argue, but he drew her out of Lola's

ELLE JAMES

house, not letting go of her hand until she climbed
into his truck.

Phoebe barely noticed how damp she still was
from cleaning up the bubble mess. Inside she was
warm and happy. She hadn't been arrested for
murder, and Nash wanted her company at lunch.
Perhaps he'd only invited her so he could keep an eye
on her. After all, she had been chased by bad guys
and discovered a body in her trunk. Now that the car
and the body were missing, he might want to stay
close and see if they turned up with her hand in the
middle of it.

Anything that might start between her and Nash
would be tainted by a murder and a theft. Until they
found the true killers, Nash would probably always
consider her a suspect. Yeah, he'd said he couldn't
imagine she had it in her to kill someone, but even
the slimmest doubt would hang over her until the
men responsible were found. She'd only known Nash
a very short amount of time. But what Nash thought
about her mattered more than she cared to admit.

Nash sat across the table from Phoebe Sinclair, the
daughter of one of the richest men in Texas, and
couldn't remember enjoying a hamburger as much.
Sure, she was high-society and way out of his league,
but then he didn't expect their lunch date to go
anywhere. It was just nice to sit across the table from

a beautiful woman who might possibly be just as messed up as he was.

He didn't like that she'd lied, but he could understand why. Who would have believed a runaway bride wasn't the prime suspect in her fiancé's murder, especially if she was carting him around in her trunk?

Thankfully, with no body, she couldn't be arrested. The fact her fiancé was dead couldn't be proven. No body, no death, no murder suspect. He stared across the table, wondering how Jonathon Sinclair's daughter had found herself in such dire circumstances and yet didn't want her daddy to bail her out.

"What?" She touched her face. "Do I have soap film on my face?"

"No." He pushed aside his empty plate. "Seems like it would be so much easier to make a phone call to your father, and you'd have everything taken care of. You wouldn't have to worry about paying rent, finding a ride or working in a bar. He could line up every lawyer and law enforcement organization in the state to keep you out of trouble."

Her lips thinned. "I'm tired of my father calling the shots for my life. I've been the good little daughter, doing everything my father and mother wanted of me, since I was born."

"But you could have everything you would ever need."

She shoved away her half-eaten hamburger. "Except self-respect and purpose. Until I worked at the Ugly Stick Saloon for one night, I didn't know what I was missing."

Nash snorted. "The Ugly Stick?"

"Yes, the Ugly Stick. I was actually *needed*. It felt good. Living with my father, the only time I've felt that way was when our stable hand took the weekend off. My father didn't know it, but I took care of the horses. For three days, they were completely dependent on me for their food and water. The work gave me a sense of purpose. At the Ugly Stick last night, I liked that I could help Audrey, the woman who'd taken a chance on me, giving me a job when I had no experience." She glanced at the clock on the wall. "Speaking of the Ugly Stick…I want to pick up some groceries and finish organizing my apartment before I go to work tonight."

Nash laid a twenty on the table, and then stood.

Phoebe pulled a wad of bills from her pocket, selected a ten and handed it to him. "For my half of the check."

He didn't argue and accepted the bill. Paying her own way seemed to be a major point in her books. If doing so made her feel more in control of her life, so be it.

As Phoebe stood beside Nash's truck, she raised her face to the bright Texas sun. "It's going to be a beautiful day." Her smile faded and she opened her eyes. "I just wish they could find whoever killed Ryan."

"Did you love him?" Nash asked, and then wished he could take back the question. He shouldn't care. But he did.

Phoebe's lips tilted upward briefly and then fell. "No. I liked him okay, and he said all the right things, but there wasn't anything else. No spark."

"Then why marry him?"

She touched Nash's chest, staring at where her fingers traced a wrinkle in his shirt. "I thought it was the right thing. Now I realize being so acquiescent was wrong in so many ways. Marriage to Ryan, had he lived, would have made us both miserable. But I didn't wish him dead, and I'm scared to think that whoever did this is still running loose."

She was so gorgeous with the sun's rays bouncing off her auburn hair, turning it a flaming copper. Nash had the sudden urge to gather her in his arms and pull her body against his. He could keep her safe, if she let him. As though drawn by an irresistible force, he leaned toward her, wanting to press his mouth to hers.

Something whizzed past his ear and pinged against the glass of the passenger seat window behind Phoebe.

Nash's gaze shifted from those tempting lips to a perfectly round hole in the glass. No sooner did it register what that hole meant than something struck his arm. He jerked at the stabbing pain.

Almost as soon as he did, Phoebe flinched and grabbed her shoulder.

"Ouch!" She glanced down at her hand. When she pulled it away from her shoulder, a bright red smear stained her palm and spread across her sleeve, where her hand had been. "What the h—"

Nash grabbed her and flung her to the ground, covering her body with his.

"What's happening?" she said, her voice muffled beneath his chest.

"Gunfire. Stay down!"

More bullets pinged against the body of his truck, putting another hole in the window, this time shattering the glass completely. Nash lay still, listening, straining to hear the weapon's report. Based on the lack of noise accompanying the shots, the weapon had to be a high-powered sniper rifle, fired from a good distance away.

"I can't breathe," Phoebe said, her voice dwindling to a whisper.

Nash eased off her body, positioning himself between Phoebe and the shooter. He eased his cell phone out of his back pocket and dialed dispatch. "Gretchen, I'm in the parking lot in front of Bob's Diner, and we have a shooter lobbing bullets at us."

"No shit!" Gretchen responded. "Stay down. I'll alert the sheriff."

"Tell him not to come to the front of the building. Seems to be us they're shooting at, but I don't want him to get caught in the crossfire."

Half a minute later, Sheriff Olson appeared around the side of the diner, weapon drawn.

By then, the gunfire had ceased.

Nash didn't feel confident it wouldn't start up again, so he remained on the ground, his body a shield protecting Phoebe.

Within the next three minutes, every sheriff's deputy on duty arrived in the parking lot, their vehicles surrounding Nash and Phoebe. The men on duty spread out on foot, searching in the direction Nash indicated from which the shots had been fired.

Nash rose to his haunches and pulled Phoebe up to hers. "Let's get inside the building."

"What's happening?" Phoebe's body trembled against his.

"I don't know, but it's not safe to remain outside in the open." He led her into the diner where they were surrounded by the staff.

Chance arrived, wearing his paramedic uniform and carrying what appeared to be his medical tool box. Within minutes, he'd cleaned and bandaged Phoebe's wound and Nash's. "You should have a doctor check them out, just in case. A tetanus shot wouldn't be a bad idea either. But from what I could tell, they are only flesh wounds. You're lucky. I saw your truck." His lips thinned into a straight line. "It could have been worse."

"Why would someone shoot at us?" Phoebe asked.

Nash shook his head. "Sweetheart, does your father have bodyguards?"

She nodded. "He does."

"Did he hire them for you?"

"I suppose."

"You don't have bodyguards here. You're exposed, and someone knows who you are. They might be targeting you because of your father." Nash frowned. "Or whoever killed your fiancé might be after you as well."

Phoebe's eyes rounded. "You could have been killed. I can't stay here." She pushed to her feet and swayed. "I can't stay in Hellfire. If I do, people could end up as collateral damage. I couldn't live with myself if you or Audrey or Lola were killed by bullets meant for me."

Nash pulled her against him. "The problem isn't *you*. It's the crazy people shooting at you."

"But they're shooting at *me*. I can't let anyone else be hurt because of me." She pressed a hand to her mouth, her eyes widening. "Do you think they killed Ryan trying to get to me?"

"I don't know." His arm firmly around her waist, he shook his head. "Until we catch them, we just have to play it safe."

Phoebe's shoulders drooped. "I have to call my father."

"Why?" Nash asked.

"He has the bodyguards, the gated estate and the money to spend tracking down the culprits."

"Or you can let the sheriff's department here in Hellfire handle this," Sheriff Olson said. "We don't like it when our citizens are threatened."

"But I'm new in town." Phoebe spoke through the tears welling in her eyes. "You can't really call me a citizen."

"Are you, or are you not, living in the apartment over Lola's garage?"

Brows wrinkled, she responded, "For an entire day. Just twenty-four hours."

"Are you gainfully employed?" the sheriff continued.

Phoebe nodded. "Yes, but—"

Sheriff raised a hand to stop her protests. "Sounds to me like you're a citizen of Hellfire. And we take care of our own." He winked and turned to Nash. "Grayson, you are officially assigned to protect Miss Sinclair until we find the man responsible for the shooting."

Nash's chest tightened, and his chin rose. Even if he hadn't been assigned, he'd have taken on the responsibility.

CHAPTER 9

"You can't do that," Phoebe said, straightening as she spoke. "I'm sure you can't afford to assign one of your men to me full time. It's not practical. My father pays a staff of security personnel. He has the money and can afford it."

"Are you living with your father?"

"Not now. But I can go back and keep you and Hellfire from having to jump through hoops to protect one person." She waved her hands in the air, feeling what little control she'd thought she had on her life slipping through her fingers. "I didn't come here to be a burden."

Sheriff Olson frowned and addressed Nash. "Deputy Grayson, do you consider protecting the citizens of Hellfire a burden?"

Nash's lips twitched. "No, sir."

"Then it's settled." The sheriff clapped his hand

onto Nash's back. "Grayson will see to it that you are safe until such a time as we find the shooter and lock him up."

This wasn't happening. The runaway train she'd been riding since she'd left the church seemed to have an endless amount of track and stops. "Seems as though I'm bad luck for Hellfire."

"You can't think that way." Sheriff Olson touched Phoebe's arm with his big callused hand. "You aren't to blame. And you don't have to give up your independence because an unidentified outlaw is gunnin' for you. We'll take care of the situation. And you."

Phoebe swallowed hard on the constriction in her throat and a tear slipped from the corner of her eye. "Thank you." She turned to Nash. "Can we go now?"

Nash nodded and hooked her elbow in his grip.

He had to be furious at the orders his boss had given. When he'd first learned she was the daughter of a wealthy man, a debutante and socialite, he'd been so angry. She'd lied to him and now he had to be her babysitter until further notice. This was not how independence was supposed to be.

Even with a parking lot full of the sheriff's department SUVs, Phoebe hesitated before stepping out of the building.

Nash circled an arm around her waist and held her close, using his body as a shield.

She wanted to push him away. Dear God, if he took another bullet meant for her...

They made it to his truck without further incident. Though the window was shattered, someone had swept the glass out of the seats. Phoebe turned her head, left and right, searching for gunmen, not really knowing where to look, or what to look for. Nash was the former soldier, surely he knew.

Nash handed her up into the truck. "You might want to sit low in the seat."

Phoebe glanced around, her jaw tight, her gaze skimming the buildings and nearby bushes and shadows. "You think they'll try to shoot me again?"

"I don't know what to think. I just know you should stay down. That way you don't make a good target."

Phoebe hunkered down, her head so low, she could barely see over the dash.

Nash got into the truck and pulled out onto Main Street. The short drive to Lola's house was accomplished in strained silence.

When he pulled into the driveway in front of her apartment, he drew in a breath, shifted the truck into Park and turned. "Gather your clothes and whatever you might need for the next few days."

"What?" With her hand on the door handle, she looked back at Nash, her eyes narrowing. Was he taking her to the nearest bus station and buying her a ticket home, just to get rid of her? "Why do I need my things?"

He pinned her with his stare. "You're coming to stay at the ranch."

Expecting the bus scenario, she took a moment before his words sunk in. Still they left her confused. "What ranch?"

"My ranch." He unbuckled his seat belt, without looking away. "The Coyote Creek Ranch. It actually belongs to my brothers and I."

Phoebe shook her head. Everything was happening too fast, leaving her thoughts spinning. "I have my own apartment. I'm not moving in with you, your brothers or anyone else."

"From what I know about your apartment, it's pretty small. Too small for the two of us."

"What two of us?" Her cheeks heated as her chest tightened. She didn't want to rely on anyone else. Taking a deep breath, she fought for calm in the face of the latest storm. "For the first time in my life, I live alone. I'm not ready to give up, yet."

The infuriating man shook his head. "Sorry, honey. You heard the sheriff. Until we catch the guy who shot at you, I'm assigned to protect you."

Phoebe crossed her arms over her chest. "I didn't leave my father's house, and his dictates, for another man to call the shots for me. This is my life, damn it!" She pounded her fist on the armrest. "I can take care of myself."

"Do you own a gun?"

She shook her head. "But I can get one."

"Do you know how to use one?"

"I've shot skeet before."

"Have you fired a handgun?" He waved his hand. "Never mind. You're in danger now. There's a waiting period to purchase weapons. You don't have the luxury of waiting for a weapon to protect yourself."

"I'm not going with you. You're not responsible for my safety." She glanced out the window. "I'll be careful."

He shoved a hand through his hair and let out a frustrated breath. "Look. I'm sorry. I didn't handle that well. I'm used to my men following my orders. I forget sometimes that I'm not in the military."

She glared at him. How was she supposed to be independent when Nash insisted on hanging around? She didn't need a man to be her bodyguard. Especially Nash Grayson. She had come to Hellfire to start over on her own. If the ruggedly handsome deputy was around day and night, she wasn't sure she could resist him. Already, she'd been close enough to kiss him, and the temptation had been almost irresistible. No. Resisting him wasn't possible.

The deputy lifted her hand in his. "Let me put it a different way."

His voice had softened until it was like warm butter seeping into every pore of her skin, igniting her senses.

"I'd be pleased..." He raised his other hand, "no...

honored, if you would allow me to protect you by staying by your side twenty-four-seven. Please, say yes. The decision will be one hundred percent yours."

For a long moment she stared at him, her eyes narrowed, her free hand fisted in her lap as she fought to keep from throwing them around his neck and kissing him. He would probably be appalled by her advances. Just because she was secretly lusting after him didn't mean he was lusting after her. Oh, hell, she was getting too deep, too fast with a man she'd only met a day before. Phoebe didn't believe in love at first sight. But lust? Oh, hell yeah. Nash Grayson was purely lust-worthy and he was staring with those incredibly blue eyes, imploring her to say yes. "I'll think about it," she finally blurted. Anything to get him to let go of her hand before she raised it to her breast and begged him to touch her any ol' way he liked, and then some.

"Be advised...If you say no to coming with me to the ranch, I'll be forced to sleep in my truck here in the driveway, to make sure you're okay. I wouldn't want you to feel bad or anything about making me sleep in this cramped, bullet-ridden vehicle." His lips twisted in a wry grin. "I'm willing to do whatever is needed to keep you safe. Even sacrifice my beauty sleep." He winked.

"I said I'd think about it." Hell, she couldn't stop thinking about him. Crammed into his truck, outside her window. Or, if she went with him to his ranch, he could be in the room beside hers, sleeping naked. Cowboys slept in the nude, didn't they? *Oh, sweet Jesus.* Was it hot inside the truck cab, or was it her? She resisted the urge to fan herself.

"Fair enough," Nash said. "Now, if you could stay put, I'll check things out." He climbed out of the truck and studied the nearby houses, the bushes, shadows and windows, probably searching for gunmen.

Phoebe could imagine him in full combat gear. Images of news reels ran through her mind of soldiers fighting battles in the desert hills of Afghanistan. Only Nash wasn't in a foreign country. Yet, he was facing a potentially hostile environment in Hellfire, Texas. Because of her.

Eventually, he opened the passenger door and helped her down from the truck. Using his body as a shield, he walked with her up the stairs to her apartment, following closely.

The entire time he hovered over her, she prayed no one would shoot. She didn't want anything to happen to Nash. He'd more than proven himself a hero by rescuing her a couple times already. He deserved a long, peaceful life. Not one peppered by bullets meant for her.

As Phoebe pressed the key into the lock, the door swung open. "What the hell?"

Nash shoved her behind him. "Let me go first. While I do...sit."

She didn't argue, just did as he said, and sat, her

hands shaking as she stared past his legs to the interior of her apartment as Nash entered.

From what she could see, boxes had been thrown, their contents spilled onto the floor. The drawers of the small kitchenette had been yanked from the cabinet, knives, forks and spoons strewn every which way.

Holy hell, what a mess. Phoebe crawled through the door and stood, her heart breaking over the damage.

Blankets and sheets of the twin bed in the corner had been ripped down the middle as though someone stabbed a sharp knife into the mattress and slashed down the center. Pillows were ripped open, the stuffing scattered like small cotton clouds. "Who would have done this?" Phoebe whispered through the hand covering her mouth.

Nash spun to face her. "I told you to wait and let me check it out."

"I'm sorry," was all she could say, tears welling in her eyes.

He shook his head and held open his arms.

Needing the reassurance of someone holding her, Phoebe walked into them. She felt as if her space had been violated. No place was sacred or safe.

"By the looks of it, someone was looking for something."

"But I don't have anything. The boxes are Lola's.

They've been here for a lot longer than I have, and nobody bothered them until I came along."

Nash smoothed a hand over her hair. "I'm betting whoever shot at you did this."

Phoebe curled her fingers into his shirt, clutching onto her sanity in the face of so much adversity. "It doesn't make sense."

"Sense or not, you aren't safe here." He tipped up her head. "You agree, don't you?"

She nodded. "How am I going to tell Lola? She took me in. Gave me a place to stay. And I repay her with a trashed apartment." She waved her hand at the boxes. "And her things have been destroyed." She couldn't stay here. Phoebe looked up at Nash, pulling her bottom lip between her teeth to keep it from trembling. She brought too much danger to the people around her. "I have to leave. I'm like a magnet for trouble."

Nash tightened his arms around her. "*You* didn't do this. Stop blaming yourself."

She couldn't meet his eyes, instead her gaze dropped to his lips. "I'm beginning to think I should just go back to my life with my father and give up on this insane notion of independence. Then, at least, no one else will be hurt."

"No one else has been hurt."

She touched his shirt where the bullet had cut a hole. "You were."

"Just a scratch." He tilted her chin upward. "You'll

be okay. We'll all be okay. Let the sheriff and his deputies handle finding the bad guys. In the meantime, I'll keep you safe."

His tone was warm, caressing, and his arms felt so strong and comforting. When Phoebe met his gaze, she melted into his blue eyes. More than her fear of bullets, she was afraid her heart wouldn't be safe from this handsome deputy. Nash didn't need her kind of complication in his life. He deserved so much better. With her breasts crushed to his chest and her hands trapped between, she couldn't fight the intense longing building inside. "Are you sure I'll be safe?" she whispered.

"I promise," Nash said. Then he lowered his head and pressed his lips to hers.

The kiss started out light, almost like an exploration of her mouth. Phoebe leaned into him, her hands climbing up his chest to circle around the back of his neck and bring him closer.

His tongue skimmed the seam between her lips and she opened to him.

At that point, something snapped between them.

Nash raised one hand to cup the back of her head, and he deepened the kiss, his tongue sweeping the length of hers, caressing, thrusting and flicking hers until she could barely think. At the same time, his other hand dug into her buttocks, pressing her belly against the hard ridge beneath the fly of his jeans.

Phoebe should have been shocked, but she wasn't.

Instead, her body burned, an ache spreading outward from her core, making her want more. She lamented the barrier of clothing separating her body from his.

When he finally raised his head, he stared downward for a long moment.

"Phoebe?" A female voice called from below. Footsteps sounded on the stairs.

Nash dropped his arms to his sides, and Phoebe stepped backward as Lola arrived in the doorway. "I don't think my kitchen floor has ever been as shiny, or my laundry room so clean as it is today—" She stopped in mid-sentence, her mouth falling open. "Oh, my God. Phoebe, darlin', are you okay?"

Phoebe struggled for words when her entire being shook with the force of her desire for the man standing so near. "I'm fine." Hell, she wasn't anywhere close to fine, and she might never be fine again. Not after that all-consuming, earth-shattering and soul-defining kiss.

NASH DROVE to the ranch in silence, still reeling. Had he known how profoundly he would be affected by one kiss, he might not have kissed Phoebe.

Who was he kidding? The more he'd been with her, the more he'd wanted to kiss her. Especially after the shooting, when Phoebe had shown her true colors. She hadn't wanted any of her newfound friends hurt because of her presence. She'd have gone back to her father's world, a world she had sworn to leave behind, just to save her adopted town from trouble.

If a body was truly in that stolen car, the murderers had killed once. They probably wouldn't stop until they killed again.

Nash's fingers tightened on the steering wheel. The sun was setting on the Texas horizon. Before he left Hellfire, he'd been in contact with the sheriff. The deputies had canvassed the area and hadn't found any mention or evidence of a sniper except for the bullets lodged in the door panel of Nash's truck. The sheriff sent them immediately to the state crime lab in Austin but it would take time before the office got anything back. Without suspects, all they could do was be on the lookout for a stranger carrying a sniper rifle.

With the tri-county rodeo still in the region, they had lots of strangers to choose from. Too many.

"I promised Charli and Libby I'd work at the Ugly Stick tonight," Phoebe said as they pulled through the gate of the Coyote Creek Ranch.

"Out of the question," Nash replied without having to think about it.

"Part of me agrees with you. The part that knows I could bring down the shooter on the patrons of the saloon. The other part wants to help them while Audrey is out of commission. She gave me a job when I needed one so badly. I hate to leave her in the lurch."

Nash shot a glance her way.

Phoebe gnawed on her lip, her brows knit in a sad kind of frown.

"Helping Audrey means a lot to you, doesn't it?" he asked.

"I told you...I want to help."

"And you feel needed." Nash could relate. Perhaps that was the reason he'd gone to work for the sheriff's office. As a soldier, he'd served his country. The ranch was a great place to go while healing his wounds, but he'd needed to be a part of something bigger than himself or the ranch. Serving the community he loved had given him back the sense of purpose and some of the camaraderie he'd lost when he'd been released from the military.

Pulling to a halt in front of the ranch house, he turned. "With this being the last night of the rodeo, the saloon will be slammed. If we're careful and you stay in the building at all times, we could go. Hopefully, the shooter won't go all postal on a crowded bar. I'll touch bases with the bouncer and have her make sure no one gets inside packing a weapon." His lips twitched. "Greta Sue can be a real ball-buster. She's not afraid of frisking people if she suspects they're carrying."

"I don't want to put anyone at risk by being there," Phoebe insisted. "I still don't understand why someone would want to kill me, or Ryan, for that matter."

"Since they tossed your apartment, they had to be looking for something."

"I had nothing on me when I left the church except my wedding dress. I was so angry when I ran out of the church, I left my purse, my wallet and identification behind."

"I don't know why you would think your fiancé would stand you up at the altar. He'd have to have been an idiot."

Phoebe smiled. "Thanks. But I don't think we really knew each other. I guess I thought he'd come to realize that and wanted out."

"But you were ready to marry him."

"I *thought* I knew him, we'd dated, even kissed on occasion. I was more interested in my horses than in whatever else was going on in my life or his. When Ryan asked me to marry him, I thought it would be nice to have a house of my own, and I've always wanted children."

Nash frowned. "You were willing to marry the man for a house and kids?"

Phoebe stared at the building in front of them. "My parents are proof you don't have to be in love to be married and procreate. Sometimes I felt like a doll they kept around to dress up and parade in front of their friends and acquaintances."

Nash shook his head, feeling sorry for the little

girl who grew up in a big house with parents who treated her as more of a possession than a cherished member of a loving family.

If she were a member of his family, he wouldn't have let her feel like a stranger in her own home. But she wasn't a member of his family. She didn't belong to him, and as soon as they found the people responsible for shooting at her, she'd no longer need him to protect her.

Though he'd only known her a day, the thought of her walking out of his life, only made him want to reach out and grab hold. The thought was insane, but he couldn't make it go away. In an attempt to direct himself away from dangerous thoughts of getting to know Phoebe better, and perhaps making her a part of his family, Nash steered the conversation in another direction. "You had horses?"

CHAPTER 10

PHOEBE SMILED across at Nash and nodded. "Yes, we had horses. I imagine my father will probably sell them, now that I'm gone."

"Neither your mother or father ride?" Nash asked.

"No. My father bought the horses as an investment. I didn't care what he called it. I was thrilled because I got to ride."

"While you're at the ranch, you can ride any horse you like."

Her chest tightened and her eyes stung. "Can I?" Why was this man so generous? She'd been nothing but trouble since he'd found her on the side of the road.

He gave her a stern look. "As long as I'm with you."

Her heart lightening, she smiled. Riding with

145

Nash sounded like heaven. "Deal. Could we ride tomorrow?"

Nash nodded, his lips curling up on the corners. "Come on. Let's see if Beckett and Kinsey are home. I don't see either one of their vehicles, but they could be parked around back."

Inside, the house was shadowed and silent.

"Beckett?" Nash called out. "Kinsey?"

No one answered.

Carrying Phoebe's plastic grocery bag full of thrift-shop clothing, Nash led the way up the stairs. "You can have this room. The bathroom is right across the hall."

"Thank you." She took the bag from his hand and laid it on the bed. "Where will you be?"

"I'm in the next room. If you run into any trouble, all you have to do is call out. I'll be there for you."

She nodded and stared around the room, glad to know Nash wouldn't be far. After all that had happened, Phoebe didn't feel safe. Her self-defense classes wouldn't help her stop a bullet, should the shooter decide to target her again.

The room she stood in was like a spread in a magazine touting the virtues of cozy cabins in the woods. A wooden four-poster bed stood in the middle of the far wall. A brightly colored quilt covered the mattress, giving the room a warm, vibrant and welcoming quality her room back home lacked.

"I'm sorry," Nash said. "It's probably not what you're used to, but it's home to us."

She turned to him, her eyes wide, tears welling. "Oh, Nash. I was just thinking how much like a real home everything here is— this room, this house, the ranch. Not like the sterile, art-deco style my mother prefers. I love it here." She wrapped her arms around his waist and pressed her cheek to his chest, inhaling the fresh outdoorsy scent that was Nash. "I'm just sorry that my bid for independence has been at the Grayson family's expense. I was supposed to live on my own, learn how to survive without my father's money or servants." She laughed and dug her fingers into his shirt, wishing she could take back all the trouble. "Instead, I'm a burden on you and your brothers."

He shifted against her, his hand resting at the small of her back, his cheek pressing against the side of her temple. "You know I don't feel that way." He tipped up her chin and stared down into her eyes. "I have to admit, when I first ran into you stranded on the side of the road, with your wedding dress puffed out all around you and your car stuck on a fencepost, I didn't expect you to stay in Hellfire." He kissed the tip of her nose. "I thought, the first chance you got, you'd be on your way back to where you'd come from."

"I couldn't go home," she admitted. "I no longer fit in there." It wasn't the first time she'd felt that way.

But this was the first time she'd done anything about it. And boy had she gone out in a big way.

Nash swept a strand of her hair back from her face, tucking it behind her ear, his coarse fingers evidence of a man who worked with his hands. As they brushed against her ear, tingles spread from where he touched on down to her aching core.

"I was certain I'd be glad to see the back of you," he whispered.

"And now?" She stared up into his clear blue gaze, her heart squeezing in her chest, her breath catching in her throat.

"I'm glad you didn't leave," he said.

Phoebe let go of the breath she'd held and leaned into his body, relieved he didn't regret meeting her.

"If you had gone," he continued, "I couldn't do this." Nash pressed his lips to her cheek and followed the line out to her earlobe.

Unable to resist his touch, Phoebe tilted her head, allowing him greater access to her bare skin.

Nash trailed kisses down the long line of her neck to the base where her pulse beat wildly. "Or this." He threaded his fingers into her thick hair and tugged her head backward. His lips found the swell of her breasts rising above the dip of the tank top neckline.

She caught the back of his neck and held his head over her breasts, her chest rising and falling like a runner at the end of a race. Each time she filled her lungs, the rounded swells rose, meeting his lips.

He graced them with a kiss, his hand sliding down her back to pull her hips closer. Nash kicked the bedroom door closed behind him.

Phoebe didn't know where his brother Beckett and his fiancée Kinsey had gone, nor when they'd be back. She didn't care. She was past thinking about anything or anyone beyond the walls of the quaint little bedroom with the pretty four-poster bed. Her focus zeroed in on the former soldier and all the naughty things he could do.

Nash squeezed the firm flesh of her buttocks.

Heat pooled low in Phoebe's belly. She wrapped one of her smooth calves around the back of his leg, her skin scraping over the denim of his jeans.

Despite the thickness of two layers of fabric between them, she could feel his heat against her center.

The hard ridge beneath his fly pressed against her leg. God, he was tempting. How could a man who'd only come into her life a day earlier have her wrapped so tightly she could barely draw a breath? With his arms around her, she could feel the hard contours of his body, her own softer curves accommodating him. Desire rose like molten lava, hot and fast, racing outward.

She hadn't come to his ranch with the intention of making love to the handsome deputy. But now, with their bodies entwined, she could think of nothing she wanted more. If she gave in to the aching passion, he'd think she was as bad as any other socialite. Still, she couldn't tear herself away. She needed him, inside her, filling her to make the emptiness of her life have new meaning. Phoebe caught his face between her hands and kissed him, her tongue pushing through his lips to tangle with his, her heart open, willing to risk everything for one chance with him.

IF HE WERE SMART, Nash would have backed up, turned and run from the room before he went any further with Phoebe. The runaway bride and daughter of the multi-millionaire was so far out of his league he would be crazy to get involved. Instead, he stood there like she was any woman, not a wealthy heiress. He held the swell of her hips in his hands, pressing her closer.

Then Phoebe pushed against his chest and stepped out of the circle of his arms.

Thank God, she was the one to break it off, to stop the insanity before they went too far. Cool air did nothing to chill the inferno blazing inside Nash. Yet, he felt bereft at the distance she'd placed between them. A moment before he'd chastised himself for letting the madness go as far as it had. Now he couldn't bring himself to let her walk away. He raised his hands to pull her back against him.

Phoebe shook her head and grasped the hem of

her tank top. With a smile, she pulled it up over her head.

Hallelujah! Nash dragged in a deep breath, closed his eyes for a moment, sending a silent 'thank you' to the heavens. Then he fought for calm, patience and whatever it would take to make him last more than five seconds before he exploded. When he opened his eyes, he took her hands and forced his gaze to rise above the lacy cups of her white, strapless bra to connect with her green-eyed stare. "I didn't bring you here to seduce you."

"Who said *you* were seducing *me?*" Smiling, she inched closer and grabbed the hem of his T-shirt. "Do you expect your brother back anytime soon?"

"God, I hope not," Nash said, his breath hitching in his chest. "You don't owe me anything."

Her brows furrowed. "Owe you?" She tilted her head sideways. "Do you think I'm paying you for rescuing me?"

He hoped not. Sex as payment for doing his job was wrong in so many ways. And what he felt for Phoebe couldn't be anything but right. "I just want to be sure."

"My father always says, nothing is sure in life, but death and taxes." She shook her head, a smile quirking the edges of her lips. "I've always followed the rules, done what I was told, thought what my father told me to think. This time, I'm thinking for myself." Her hands twisted in his shirt and dragged it upward, inch by inch. "I want to feel for myself and... make love to the one *I* want." She stopped halfway up his torso. "Unless, you don't want to." Her eyes shot wide. "Good Lord, I don't want to take advantage of you, any more than I already have."

"Advantage of me...not want to?" He couldn't wrap his thoughts around her words. They made absolutely no sense, and the pretty frown settling between her eyes only made him laugh. "Are you kidding?" He pulled her hips toward him and nudged her belly with the hard ridge beneath his jeans. "What do you think?"

Her frown disappeared, and she slid her hand between them, cupping his package. "I think we're heading in the same direction."

"Good, because I was beginning to think I'd fallen down a rabbit hole with no directions for how to get out." With a quick move, he yanked his shirt over his head and tossed it to the corner.

Phoebe squeezed his hand and backed toward the bed. "This way, Alice."

He resisted, shaking his head. "You did *not* just call me Alice."

Phoebe winked. "If not Alice, show me who you are." Holding his gaze, she reached for the rivet on her denim shorts and flicked it open. When her fingers closed around the metal zipper tab, she smiled and drew it downward.

Blood roared in Nash's ears and thundered

through his veins, heading due south. He swept Phoebe up by the backs of her thighs and lifted, wrapping her long, luscious legs around his waist. His cock strained against the confines of his jeans, aching to press into the warm wetness of her channel.

Dipping his head, he claimed her mouth, plundering its depths, tasting and teasing her tongue until she clamped her hands around his head and gave as good as she got. Nash crossed the floor and eased Phoebe onto the bed, knocking the bag of her clothes to the floor. "Say the word and we can stop here."

"For the love of Mike, don't stop now." She weaved her hands into his hair and pulled him closer, making room for him on the bed beside her.

Nash pulled his wallet from his back pocket, extracted a condom and laid it on the bed beside her. "I was a good boy scout. Always prepared."

"Oh, thank God. I didn't even think…" Phoebe mumbled and grabbed his shoulders, rolling him onto his back. She shimmied out of her shorts, kicked them to the floor and straddled his hips to tug at the button on his jeans.

He covered her hands with his. "Why the hurry?"

"Seriously?" She stared at him, her jaw dropping. "I'm on fire! If we wait one more minute, I'm certain the sheets will spontaneously combust. I won't be held responsible if your house burns down because you wanted to waste time on foreplay."

At her unexpected comment, he laughed out loud. His chest tight, his groin tighter, Nash sobered, leaned forward and kissed her, then flipped her onto her back and pressed his lips to the hammering pulse at the base of her throat. He edged lower, pushing aside the cup of her bra to capture a nipple between his teeth. "You're beautiful."

Phoebe gasped. She arched her back, offering up more of herself, twisting an arm behind her back to unhook the bra. "Enough talk." Both breasts sprang free, lush, perky and tipped with rosy peaked nipples.

Nash sucked one into his mouth, taking as much as he could, flicking and tapping the hardening evidence of her desire.

She clasped his head and shifted his attention to the other one.

After thoroughly exploring the second perfectly formed nipple, Nash blazed a path downward, his mind completely consumed by the image of her body lying against his grandmother's quilt, the brightly-colored squares framing her in a cacophony of color and light.

Her bright, coppery hair spilled out around her shoulders, her green eyes reflecting the sunlight filtering through the open window. "Please," she moaned.

"Please what?"

"I want you…nooowww." She ran her hand down her belly to cup the juncture of her thighs.

Nash hooked his thumb in the elastic of her panties, dragged the scrap of silk down her legs, past her feet and tossed it to the corner. He rolled off the bed, shucked his boots and jeans, all the while consuming her with his gaze. When he stood before her naked, he couldn't believe this beautiful woman, with the pale skin, flaming auburn hair, and eyes the color of spring hay, lay waiting for him.

Phoebe's cheeks flushed a pretty pink. "You look like you're hungry and ready to eat the proffered offering."

"I am, and I will."

Her eyes darkened. She drew her knees upward and then let them fall to each side, leaving a gap between her legs for him to slide between.

And he did. Climbing onto the bed, he settled between her legs, draping her thighs over his shoulders. He scooped his hands beneath her bottom and raised her to him.

Her entrance glistened with the dew of her desire. She dug her hands into the quilt, curling her fingers around the colorful squares.

Nash dipped his tongue into her center and swirled.

Phoebe threw back her head and moaned.

He chuckled. "Still think I'm wasting time on foreplay?"

"No!" she said, her voice barely more than a gasp. "Yes! No!"

Nash loved that she was conflicted. Loved that she was overcome by her passion. Not until he brought her to the very edge would he take her. Not a moment sooner. Their first time had to be so incredible, she would stay for another...and another.

He continued to tongue her until she twisted her hands in his hair, arched her back and cried out, "I need you. Inside me. Now!"

He climbed up between her legs, applied the condom and entered her slowly, letting her adjust to his size.

Her channel contracted around him, squeezing, drawing him deeper.

The heat, the slick moisture and her legs wrapping around him pushed him past his ability to take his time and make it last. "I. Can't. Hold. Back. Any longer."

She clasped his face in her hands and stared up into his eyes. "Then don't. Give me all you've got."

He thrust into her, hard, fast and deep, pounding against her again and again.

Phoebe threw back her head and moaned. She lowered her legs, dug her heels into the mattress and met him thrust for thrust.

The closer he came to the edge of release, the more rigid his body grew. Driving into her one last time, he launched into the stratosphere, calling out her name. "Phoebe! Oh, sweet Phoebe!"

He remained deep inside her for a long, exquisite

moment, his cock throbbing, the tension leaving him with each passing second. Finally, he collapsed on the bed beside her, maintaining their intimate connection.

Now that he'd had her in his arms and buried himself inside her, he couldn't let her go. He wanted to get to know this woman who'd turned her back on her life in the city, with servants taking care of her every need, to start over in Hellfire.

Nash prayed she didn't change her mind. Following his first prayer, he asked to keep her safe from the men who'd attacked her. He hoped he would be smart and brave enough to deflect any future attempts on Phoebe's life.

CHAPTER 11

PHOEBE SNUGGLED against Nash for over an hour, reveling in the warmth and security of his muscled chest and rock-hard biceps. Skin to skin, she'd never felt more beautiful or cherished. In the back of her mind, she knew she should feel guilty that she was in another man's bed barely a day after the death of her fiancé.

But she couldn't feel the guilt. Only sorrow for a life ended before his time. Now that she knew what real passion was, Phoebe realized she'd never felt more than a brotherly liking for Ryan. Even that feeling had been a product of her father's encouragement and approval of the match. She'd been stupid to agree to the wedding in the first place, when she didn't love the man she was to marry.

She ran her hand across Nash's broad chest, feeling the strength of his muscles beneath skin stretched tightly over his frame. This was a man she could fall in love with. Nash was a veteran, a man of honor who'd fought for his country and now served his community as a deputy, making it a safer place to live. And he protected her from a man who'd been determined to put a bullet through her.

As a shiver rippled across her body, she fingered her grandmother's locket at her throat. If the shooter's aim had been a little more to the right, Nash might have been killed.

His arm tightened around her. "Are you cold?"

"No." For a moment, she pressed her cheek to his chest then she pushed up enough to look into his eyes. "But I need to get ready to work at the saloon tonight."

"Or you could call Audrey and tell her you can't make it."

Phoebe bit down on her bottom lip. "Remember, she hurt herself last night. If I don't show up, she might decide she needs to be there and rip a stitch or something."

Nash leaned up and kissed the tip of her nose. "Then you'd better get ready. You can have the first shower."

"I have a better idea." She rolled off the bed, took his hand and tipped her head toward the door. "Why don't we shower together?"

With a grin spreading across his face, Nash leaped out of the bed, snatched a second condom from his wallet and hurried for the door. He opened it and stuck out his head. "Beckett? Kinsey?"

No one answered.

"Come on." Holding her hand, he led her across the hall to the bathroom.

Phoebe smothered a giggle and closed the door behind them. Once in the shower, the giggles continued as she chased the bar of soap around, bumped into all parts of Nash and sloshed water all over the floor. In between playing, they made love again.

Nash lifted her up, wrapped her legs around his waist and braced her against the cool tiled wall. Nothing could chill the heat from her body, not when Nash sheathed himself and drove deep inside her. She'd never felt so incredible. As Nash thrust into her, Phoebe shot into the heavens on the best orgasm she'd ever experienced.

He held her there, buried deep inside until they both returned to earth under the cooling spray of the shower. Nash eased her to her feet, rinsed her body, and then shut off the water.

Phoebe rose up on her toes and pressed a kiss to his lips. He held her wet body against his. She loved his hard, muscular chest and the steely strength of his arms.

As much as she'd rather go right back to bed with Nash, Phoebe had a promise to keep. She reached for a towel and dried Nash's body as he dried hers.

More laughter ensued until they stood dry and breathless.

"Hey, everything okay in there?" a deep voice called out.

Gaze narrowed, Nash pressed a finger to her lips. "I'm fine. Just fine."

Phoebe kissed his finger, swallowing another giggle. Who knew making love could be so much fun?

"I'm not worried about you. I'm concerned about the woman you're holding prisoner in there," Beckett said. "Knock three times if you're being held against your will."

Phoebe gasped and answered, "I'm fine, too."

"Good," Beckett said with a chuckle. "I was afraid I'd have to call the cops on my cop brother."

"Jerk." Nash shook his head, a smile pulling at his lips.

"Damn right," Becket returned. "One of us has to keep a level head. As the oldest, I feel like it's my responsibility."

Nash rolled his eyes. "We're going to the Ugly Stick again tonight, if you and Kinsey want to join us."

"I think we'll pass on the saloon. Shower sex sounds like more fun."

"Beckett!" Kinsey cried out. "You don't have to announce our *plans* to the world."

"You mean our plans to have sex in the shower?"

Beckett laughed out loud. A loud smacking sound followed. "Ouch! You didn't have to hit me that hard."

"Quit crying, baby. And leave those two alone."

"I take it Phoebe's not changing her mind about getting married since the groom is apparently dead." Beckett's voice moved away from the door. "Oh, by the way, in case you haven't heard, they found the car and the body in the trunk."

Nash wrapped a towel around his waist and yanked open the door. "What did you say?"

Gasping, Phoebe tucked a towel around her body and leaned around Nash to see Beckett and Kinsey standing in the hallway.

Beckett nodded. "Got your attention, finally." He tipped his head toward Kinsey. "We were in the diner when Sheriff Olson got the call."

"Where did they find it?" Nash asked.

"In the old gravel quarry east of town. That poor car is completely totaled. From what the sheriff said, whoever stole it ripped up every seat and tore out the door panels and headlining. Then, they burned it."

Phoebe reeled backward, the blood rushing from her head into the pit of her belly.

"Thanks for letting me know."

"You would probably know if you'd answered your phone." Beckett's lips twisted into a wry grin. "Of course, answering your phone when you're having sex in the shower with a beautiful woman can be difficult."

Kinsey backhanded Beckett in the belly. "You've teased them enough."

Beckett winked at Nash. "That's my cue to shut up and put up."

Kinsey took his hand and led him toward the master suite, calling out over her shoulder, "If you need us, you know where you can find us."

Nash waited until Beckett and Kinsey disappeared behind the master suite door before leading Phoebe back to the bedroom across the hallway. As soon as she crossed the threshold, Phoebe clutched her belly, a sick, awful feeling forming. "If they have the body, they now have reason to take me in on suspicion of murder." She turned to face him. "Oh, my God. Nash, you just made love with a potential murder suspect. What will happen to you? What will we do?"

NASH'S GUT TIGHTENED. He didn't give a damn that Phoebe's dead fiancé had shown up. Deep down, he knew Phoebe didn't have a mean bone in her body. She couldn't have killed the man, and she sure as hell couldn't have stuffed his body in the trunk. "What we're doing is continuing on as though nothing happened. You're going to work at the Ugly Stick and I'll go along to keep you safe. Just like the sheriff ordered." He tipped his head toward her towel. "You might want to put on some clothes. I know they prefer the girls show some skin, but you're a little underdressed even for Ugly Stick standards."

Phoebe yanked off her towel and popped him with it.

He tackled her on the bed and ended the argument with a deep, soul-wrenching kiss. When he finally came up for air, he wanted nothing more than to remain in the bed, making love to Phoebe through the night.

She stared up into his eyes. "What happens next?"

He knew she wasn't asking about getting dressed and going to work. "Let the sheriff decide. They will probably take me off the case due to conflict of interest."

She curled her fingers around his arms. "Will the sheriff remove you from bodyguard duty?"

"He might." Nash rose from the bed and held out his hand. Not that he'd obey an order to stand down from his duties as bodyguard to Phoebe. He couldn't imagine leaving her unprotected, or entrusting her safety to someone else.

Phoebe placed her hand in his and let him pull her to her feet.

Nash enveloped her in his embrace and held her naked body against his, his cock nudging her belly, ready for another round of lovemaking. "We'll figure out this thing."

Nestling close, she wrapped her arms around his waist. "I hope so." Then she straightened and smiled, though her lips appeared a little tight and strained. "Right now, I'd better get dressed for the Ugly Stick." Phoebe pulled on the cut-off denim shorts and tank top she'd worn earlier and the cowboy boots she'd found at the thrift shop.

While she ran a brush through her damp, auburn curls, Nash dressed in his jeans and pulled on his boots. By the time he was ready, she was standing at the door, her hand on the doorknob.

"Just so you know, just because we engaged in..." Her cheeks burned a bright red as she glanced around the room, as if searching for the right word.

"Lovemaking?"

Her gaze anchored on his. "Sex." She pushed back her shoulders. "You're not in any way under any obligation to me."

He stiffened. "Is this your way of giving me the brush-off?"

Her eyes widened. "On the contrary. I'm giving you permission to walk away. No strings attached."

Fighting anger at her dismissal, he closed the distance and pulled her into his arms. "I'd rather have your permission to take you on a date. To get to know you better."

She snorted softly. "I'd say you know me better already than any of my family." She rested a hand on his chest. "I just don't want you to ruin your reputation with a murder suspect. You deserve better than that."

"And you deserve to live your life as you see fit."

"If I'm arrested, I might have to get my father to bail me out of this mess. Without him, I don't have access to the best lawyers money can buy. Heck, I don't even have the funds for the *worst* lawyers money can buy."

"Hopefully, the situation won't come to that." He tried to pull her close to kiss her one more time.

Her hand on his chest firmed, and she held him off. "Promise me you won't let anyone know we had a fling. I couldn't bear it if you were dragged into this mess."

"Only if you promise to go out with me when the dust settles." He brushed a strand of her hair behind her ear, loving how soft and silky it felt. He didn't like that Phoebe was trying to protect him, when he was supposed to be protecting her.

"Deal." She held out her hand.

He took it in his and shook before lifting it to his lips. "You're an amazing woman, Phoebe. Don't disappear on me when I'm just getting to know you." Nash pressed a kiss to the back of her hand. With a slight tug, he pulled her against him and claimed her mouth in one last, desperate kiss. Something inside him told him it might be just that. The last kiss.

They left the house and climbed into his truck, heading for the county line where the Ugly Stick Saloon sat at the convergence of three counties. The parking lot was filled and overflowing with pickup trucks, SUVs and dusty cowboys.

Nash walked Phoebe past the rowdy bunch of men there to celebrate after a hard, hot day at the rodeo.

They entered through the front door, and Greta Sue, the bouncer built like a freight train, stepped in front of them. "Is that a banana in your pocket, or you just glad to see me?"

Nash leaned close and opened his jacket enough for Greta Sue to see the Glock tucked in a shoulder holster. "On duty, Greta Sue," he whispered.

Her eyes narrowed. "I heard about the shooting earlier today." Her gaze shifted to Phoebe. "Glad you're taking care of our girl." She stepped aside, allowing them to proceed.

Phoebe's lips curled into a smile, her eyes filling with tears.

"What's wrong?" Nash asked.

"Nothing. Everything's great." She glanced up at him, letting her smile spread across her face. "For the first time in my life, I just feel like I belong. It's a good feeling."

Nash's heart squeezed in his chest at the look of joy on Phoebe's face. She must have led a pretty lonely life in the city, despite all the people around her. Well, not anymore. She was one of them now.

Once inside, Phoebe went right to work, carrying trays of drinks to thirsty patrons.

Nash stood against the wall and waited for a seat at the bar to open, his gaze darting between the bar and Phoebe as she wove her way through the tables and cowboy boots, smiling and happy serving others. He could hardly believe she was the daughter of a multi-millionaire. She wasn't at all concerned about serving others or breaking a nail. She wasn't above the cowboys in their worn jeans and scuffed boots. She wore second-hand clothes and was damn proud to have them.

"She's doing great," a voice said beside him.

He turned to face Audrey, wearing a white blouse, a pair of jeans and her signature red cowboy boots with metal studs. "I thought you would be home with your leg up, babying your stitches."

"I had to do some fancy talking to get Jackson to bring me. I told him I was uncomfortable lying down and standing was better. I also promised not to stay too long." She spread her hands wide. "As you can see, they don't need me anyway."

"They will always need you, sweetheart." Jackson joined them. "You're what makes this place so great."

"Damn right she is," Nash agreed.

Audrey's face reddened. "Thanks."

For another minute, the three of them stood in silence. Nash couldn't take his gaze from Phoebe. Something about the way she moved mesmerized him and made him count the minutes until he could get her back to the ranch house and in his bed. He hadn't been looking for a woman to share his life, and he never thought the runaway bride he'd found on the road into Hellfire would be the one for him, but now…

"She's a beautiful woman, our Phoebe," Audrey said. "And she fits right in at the Ugly Stick. She's smart, quick on her feet and has such a welcoming smile." The owner of the saloon bumped shoulders with Nash. "You like her, don't you?"

Nash stiffened. Were his feelings for Phoebe that obvious? "She's okay."

"You wouldn't be hanging around so much, if you didn't." Audrey persisted.

He didn't tell her what he knew about Phoebe and that Sheriff Olson had assigned him to protect the socialite.

"You don't have to tell me anything about Phoebe, I have my sources." Audrey crossed both arms over her chest. "You'd never guess she was the daughter of the Dallas billionaire Jonathon Sinclair." Her smile faded, and she laid a hand on Nash's arm. "I also know someone is after her, and that someone fired on you two earlier today. I'm glad neither of you were hurt."

Nash shot a glance down at Audrey. "She almost didn't come to work tonight, because she was afraid she'd bring trouble to the saloon."

"I'm glad she came. I can't get around easily to

help out. Enough people are in the place that I doubt the shooter would try to get to her here."

"Come on, darlin'," Jackson said. "Let's get you off your feet. The doctor won't be happy if he finds out you came to work."

Audrey frowned and rubbed the sides of her jeans. "I guess you're right. My stitches are rubbing against the denim."

Jackson winked. "Let's get you home and naked where you can heal properly."

Her eyes lit, and she turned into her husband's arms. "Or we could get naked in the storeroom and count whiskey bottles or whatever else you had in mind."

The pair was notorious for getting it on in the storeroom. After being together for a couple years and having a baby, they still acted like newlyweds who couldn't get enough of each other.

Nash fought the grin threatening to spread across his face as Audrey led Jackson to the storeroom.

Shaking his head, Jackson protested, "We need to take this home where you don't have to get dressed afterward."

"Come on, big guy. I can't wait that long." Audrey didn't look back, tugging him by the hand to the back of the building.

Nash's attention returned to Phoebe who was waving from the bar. A stool had opened, and she sat in it to keep someone else from taking over.

Hurrying across the floor, he arrived in time to kiss her soundly for saving him a spot.

Then she was back on the floor with a tray full of mugs and whiskey shooters.

"Hey."

A commotion at the entrance made Nash rise from his seat, his hand on the gun tucked beneath his jacket. Two men in dark suits lifted Greta Sue by her arms and physically moved her out of the way.

Then a loud, booming voice called out over the music and laughter, "Phoebe Sinclair!"

The band stopped playing, and every gaze turned toward the man bellowing like a bull in a field full of heifers.

"Phoebe Sinclair, I will have words with you, young lady."

Nash shot a glance toward Phoebe as the tray she'd been carrying tilted sideways and the empty mugs and bottles slipped off, landing with a crash on the floor.

She stood still, her face losing all its color, her teeth chewing on her bottom lip. "Daddy?"

CHAPTER 12

PHOEBE HEARD her father's voice, and her knees wobbled and the tray she'd been carrying tilted. Before she could do anything to stop gravity from taking its due, everything she'd been carrying crashed to the floor. She spun to face the angry face of her father, the well-known entrepreneur and multi-millionaire, Jonathon Sinclair. "Daddy?"

"Phoebe Rochelle Sinclair, what the hell do you mean by running out on your wedding with a church packed full of people?"

Every face turned from her father toward her.

If she could have, she would have sunk through the floor. But she couldn't, and she'd never have her independence if she didn't stand up to her father and make her own wishes known. Stiffening her spine, she tilted her chin high. "I can't marry Ryan."

"After all the money I spent on the ceremony and

all the people we invited to watch my only daughter marry, why the hell not?" His words shook the timbers holding up the metal roof over their heads.

"For one...I never loved him." Her gaze turned of its own accord to the tall man standing at the bar, his hand inside his jacket, ready to take on anyone who threatened her. Including her father.

Nash's jaw was set in a tight line and his brows dipped low over narrowed eyes.

Just his being there gave Phoebe the strength she needed to confront her overbearing father. She faced the man who'd raised her. "And for the second reason, Ryan's dead." For the first time in her life, Phoebe saw surprise on her father's face.

"Dead? What do you mean dead?"

"As in no longer breathing."

"You killed your fiancé?" Her father ran a hand through his hair, a frown pressing his bushy brows together. Then he straightened to his full, intimidating height of six feet four inches. "I'll hire the best defense team the world has seen since the O.J. Simpson trials. It had to be self-defense. What did that man do to you?"

Surely he didn't believe she'd kill a man. Her father really didn't know his own daughter. Phoebe held up her hands. "No, Daddy, I didn't kill Ryan, but someone did. I just happened to leave the wedding in his car. Unbeknownst to me, he was already dead and in the trunk."

Her father looked around the barroom at all the faces of silent patrons staring from him to his daughter and back. "What are you all looking at? Can't a man have a private conversation with his daughter without people gawking? Go back to what you were doing, for Pete's sake." To Phoebe, he said, "Come on, girl. Let's go home and figure this out."

This was it—the confrontation. Phoebe crossed her arms over her chest and stood with her feet slightly parted, ready to take on anyone who tried to force her to leave. "I'm not going with you, Daddy."

One cowboy turned to Phoebe. "That's right, Phoebe, don't let him push you around. We've got your back. You're one of us now." The man stood and planted himself in front of her father.

Jonathon Sinclair was a man used to getting his way. He glared at the cowboy but waved to his bodyguards. "Get her."

Several cowboys stood, blocking the bodyguards from advancing toward Phoebe.

Nash crossed to where she stood and slipped an arm around her waist. "Mr. Sinclair, your daughter has made her home in Hellfire. She won't be leaving with you."

"Get your hands off my daughter," her father demanded. "She's coming home."

"Not if she doesn't want to." He moved to stand slightly in front of Phoebe.

"Watch it, boy, or I'll have you up on kidnapping charges."

"He didn't kidnap me, Daddy," Phoebe said. "No one forced me to leave the church or to stay in Hellfire. I left because I want to live my own life, make my own decisions and choose the man I want to spend the rest of my life with."

"Don't be ridiculous. You belong in Dallas, not this backwater small town with nothing but a bunch of hicks who have nothing better to do with their lives than drink beer."

Every cowboy and all of the women in the saloon stood and faced Phoebe's father.

Anger surged through Phoebe at her father's rude words. These people had been good to her. They'd taken her in when she didn't have a place to stay, made sure she had clothes to wear and a place to work. "Daddy, if you ever want to see me again, you'll apologize to the men and women in this saloon."

"I will not."

Phoebe tapped her toe on the wooden floor. "Then please leave. I don't want to see you ever again."

Glancing around, he drew in a long breath and huffed it out. "You can't be serious."

"I am."

"Then don't expect me to pay for your lawyers when you're arrested for murder."

Her stomach sank, but she refused to let her

father push her around ever again. "I'll manage on my own."

"You'll be trading in your Gucci for prison orange, I tell you."

She swept a hand down her torso and the second-hand clothes. "Does this outfit look like Gucci?"

His gaze raked her from head to toe. "No, but what you're wearing really isn't the point. Without my lawyers, you don't stand a chance."

Phoebe shrugged. "So be it."

"Damn it, Phoebe, don't be stubborn!" her father shouted, his hands fisted at his sides.

She raised her brows, her lips quirking on the corners. "I come by it honestly."

Her father's eyes narrowed to a squint. For a long moment, he stared across the room full of cowboys. "Fine. Have it your way." He turned to the men in the room. "I'm sorry."

Phoebe's fists tightened. "Say it like you mean it."

"Isn't it enough I apologized?" he implored. "I never apologize."

"Yes, you apologized, but you didn't sound at all sincere." She softened her voice. "Daddy, it's never too late to be kind."

Jonathon Sinclair stared again at the sea of faces. Finally, his shoulders relaxed and he chuckled. "She's a lot more like me than I gave her credit." He tipped his head toward the crowd and spoke in a sincere voice. "Please, accept my most sincere apology. You are all fine men and women, and it was arrogant of me not to recognize and appreciate you for who you are." He held their attention for another long moment, and then turned to Phoebe. "Now, will you come with me?"

"First of all, I shouldn't have had to tell you that you were being rude. Second, I'm still not leaving. I have a job, and you're in the way of these hardworking, thirsty men." Phoebe winked at the patrons.

The occupants of the saloon raised their voices in loud yee-haws and resumed their seats.

Phoebe fought the grin threatening to spread across her face and waved over her father. "If you're staying, you have to order something. What can I get you?"

Her father glanced around, a smile curling his lips. "It's been a long time since I've been in a bar as rustic as this. How about a Budweiser?"

"I'll bring you a Light." Phoebe patted her father's protruding belly. "You're supposed to be on a diet."

He stood taller. "Are you a waitress or a daughter?"

"Both." She faced the bodyguards. "Diet soda for you, Frank? Ginger ale for Smitty?"

They nodded and stood on either side of her father.

Phoebe shook her head. "Oh, for heaven's sake, sit."

All three men grabbed a chair and sat.

Empowered by having her commands followed, Phoebe turned toward the mess on the floor.

Nash squatted beside the broken mugs and bottles, loading them onto the tray. "I've got this." He looked up at her and smiled. "By the way, you're amazing."

Phoebe nodded and grinned. "Damn right, I am." And Nash was equally amazing and supportive of her attempt to start a new life. With starch in her spine and hope filling her heart, she marched toward the bar and ordered the drinks.

"Uh, Phoebe?" a voice called out behind her.

Audrey stood in the shadow of the hallway leading to the back of the building. The light bulb must have burned out because the corridor was darker than usual. Audrey's usual happy face was pale and tense. She held her arm behind her back at an awkward angle.

"Audrey?" Phoebe hurried toward her boss. "Are you all right?"

The strawberry-blonde shook her head. "Not really." Tears trickled from the corners of her eyes.

As Phoebe neared the saloon owner, she could see why. Her breath hitched and a lead weight settled in the pit of her stomach.

A man stood behind her, a ski mask covering his face. "Keep quiet, and do as I say, or I hurt the woman."

He eased his hand from behind Audrey enough

for Phoebe to see the gun in his grip. A taller man stood behind the first. With both of them dressed in black, they could barely be seen in the darkened hallway.

"They hit Jackson in the head. He's lying on the floor in the storeroom."

The man holding her jerked her arm back farther.

Audrey winced. "I don't care about me, but Jackson…"

The man holding Audrey tipped his head. "Come with us."

Blood pounding in her ears, Phoebe glanced over her shoulder.

Nash straightened, his gaze going to the bar.

"Now," the man said. "Or I hurt the pretty lady."

Phoebe stepped into the dark hallway, praying Nash saw her as she did. As her bodyguard, he would follow her, even if she was only talking to Audrey.

The men didn't stop until they pushed through the back exit.

Once the door closed behind Phoebe, she planted her feet on the ground and demanded, "What do you want?"

The taller man pointed a gun at Phoebe. "We want what Bratton gave you."

Phoebe shook her head. "I don't know what you're talking about."

"The code," said the man holding Audrey. "We

want the code to the account where he moved the money."

Her heart hammering, Phoebe glanced from one of the men to the other. Audrey was clearly in distress, Jackson lay injured in the storeroom, and these men wanted something she knew nothing about. Eager to do whatever it took to get these men to leave, she asked, "What code? What money?"

"Don't play dumb, little rich bitch. We know he gave it to you. It wasn't in the car, and he didn't have it on his body when we stiffed him," said the man holding the gun on her.

The one holding Audrey continued, "We searched your suitcases back at the church and it wasn't in either one."

"So he had to have given it to you. He planned to take it on your honeymoon to the Cayman Islands, withdraw the money from the bank and disappear."

Phoebe's heart hardened. Ryan, the bastard, really did deserve to die. But she refused to be collateral damage to his dirty deal. "That's news to me. He didn't clue me in on his plan."

"He had to have. Otherwise, why did you leave?"

Audrey caught Phoebe's attention, mouthing the word "one."

Phoebe tensed when Audrey mouthed the word "two."

On "three," Audrey slammed her elbow into the

midsection of the man holding her and dove out of range of his gun then scrambled to her feet.

Phoebe put her self-defense lessons to use and threw a sidekick into the other man's hand, knocking the gun from his grip. She shoved the man who'd held Audrey into the man behind him and ran.

Limping, Audrey made it around the corner, but Phoebe had only gone a couple yards when someone hit her from behind and sent her sprawling face-first into the dirt. A hand grabbed her long hair and yanked so hard, she thought for sure a hank would come loose. The man who'd tackled her leaned close to her ear and breathed fetid breath into the side of her face.

"Move another muscle, and I'll kill you, like I killed your fiancé."

NASH STRAIGHTENED with the tray full of broken glass, satisfied he'd gotten all of the pieces so no one would be cut by the jagged shards. Immediately, his gaze sought Phoebe. She wasn't at the table with her father and his bodyguards.

Turning toward the bar, he didn't see her with Libby, the bartender, filling drink orders. His pulse kicked up a notch, but he wasn't too concerned. She could be behind the counter, helping unload a box of whiskey, or she could have gone to the storeroom for a case of beer.

Nash carried the tray to the bar. "Have you seen Phoebe?"

Libby pulled the tap, filling a mug with beer. "Audrey called her to the storeroom, I think. Want me to go look? I could use a case of whiskey."

"No. I'll go check." Nash hurried to the hallway leading to the storeroom. He couldn't remember it being as dark as it was. He flipped the switch on the wall. The lights came on, and he entered the storeroom. "Phoebe?" he called out. Rows of boxes were stacked high enough he couldn't see around them.

A moan rose from behind the stack.

Nash's heartbeat thundered against his ribs as he ducked around the boxes to find Jackson Gray Wolf laying with his face on the ground, a bloody lump forming at his temple. "Jackson?" Nash knelt beside the man.

Jackson rolled onto his back and stared up at Nash. "Where's Audrey?"

"I was going to ask you the same. What happened?"

"Don't know." He pushed to a sitting position and held onto his head. "I was kissing my wife when someone hit me." He looked into Nash's face and his eyes widened. "Audrey." Jackson staggered to his feet.

Nash steadied him.

"Don't worry about me, find Audrey. Whoever hit me might have taken her."

She wasn't in the bar. Not in the storeroom. She had to have gone out the back door.

Nash sprinted for the door.

Hands on hips, Greta Sue stood in the hallway. "You're in a restricted area."

"Greta Sue." Jackson leaned in the doorway behind Nash. "Audrey's in trouble."

The big woman's eyes grew round. "Where is she?"

"We don't know," Nash said. "Get Phoebe's father and his bodyguards and head out the front. Jackson and I are headed out the back." He darted for the back exit. "And have Libby call 911," he called out over his shoulder.

Without waiting for Jackson, Greta Sue or Phoebe's father and his bodyguards, Nash hit the back door and leaped off the landing onto the ground.

A man wearing a ski mask ran toward the side of the building.

"Hey!" Nash shouted.

The man turned, and a shot whizzed past Nash's head.

Nash dove and rolled to his feet, pulling his Glock from the holster beneath his jacket as he came up.

At that moment, Jackson slammed open the back door, drawing attention away from Nash.

The man in the ski mask swung his arm toward Jackson.

Nash fired, hitting the man square in the chest, dropping him where he stood.

A car engine revved at the side of the building, backed up to where the man lay on the ground and then shot forward.

Audrey staggered from around the side of the building, a hand braced against the structure. "The other guy has Phoebe. Don't let him take her."

Nash dodged around Audrey, focusing all his energy into catching up to that car and rescuing his runaway bride, yet again. He couldn't let someone hurt her now. In the short amount of time he'd known her, he had fallen under her spell. He couldn't let it end here. He wouldn't.

The sedan pulled away, spitting up gravel as it swerved to avoid hitting a truck backing out of a parking space. As it pulled around the backing truck, the sedan hit another truck's tailgate then spun sideways, the front of the sedan stuck to the tailgate. The sedan's driver backed away, but couldn't shake loose from the tailgate. He dragged the truck a few inches and then stopped, the tires of the sedan spinning in the gravel, going nowhere.

Nash didn't dare shoot the driver when he couldn't see where he had Phoebe. Instead, he raced for the sedan and reached for the driver's door and yanked it open.

Inside, a man wearing a ski mask cursed. With one hand on the steering wheel, he held a gun in his other hand, pointing at Phoebe who was tipped sideways against the passenger door, her arms and feet bound in duct tape. "Touch me," the driver warned, "and I'll blow her head off."

"The hell you will," Phoebe said. She lifted her bound legs and kicked the man's wrist, sending the gun flying across the seat. Then she kicked again, landing both of her feet in the side of the man's face. "That's for hurting my new friends." She would have kicked him again.

Nash grabbed the man, yanked him out of his seat and threw him onto the ground. When he tried to get up on his hands and knees to scramble away, Nash dropped on top of him, pressing his knee into the small of the man's back. He held his gun to the man's head. "Move, and I'll blow *your* head off," he said, repeating the same words the man had used to threaten Phoebe.

Sirens wailed in the distance, and footsteps crunched in the gravel beside him.

Phoebe's father appeared with his bodyguards and Greta Sue. They helped Phoebe out of the car and carefully removed the duct tape from her arms and legs.

By the time the sheriff arrived, the entire saloon had emptied, gathering around Phoebe, Audrey, Nash and Jackson. A fire truck arrived, and Chance climbed down and pushed through the crowd to check over the four of them. He pronounced them fit, with the caveat that Jackson go to the emergency room in case he had a concussion and subsequent swelling in the brain.

Sheriff Olson took possession of the prisoner. "I take it these are the guys who killed Ryan Bratton, the man in the trunk of the car Miss Sinclair brought to Hellfire?"

Phoebe nodded and pointed. "This one admitted to killing Ryan."

"My word against hers," the man said with a shrug.

Audrey came to stand beside her. "I will testify I heard him say he killed Phoebe's fiancé."

Phoebe's attacker glared at Audrey. "I want a lawyer."

"Looks like we have a murder suspect." Sheriff Olson cuffed the man, put him in the back of his service vehicle and then returned to Phoebe and Nash. "Guess your bodyguard duties are done, Grayson."

Mr. Sinclair turned to Nash and held out his hand. "Thank you for taking care of my baby girl." He shook his head. "I might be a big ol' grouch and a bit pushy, but I love that girl."

Phoebe hooked her arm through Nash's. "If you love me, then let me live my life the way I see fit."

Nash's chest swelled at Phoebe's demand. She could have everything handed to her on a silver platter if she returned to her father's house. But she chose independence. And by the way she was holding onto his arm, she was choosing to stay with him.

Her father nodded. "Seems you're a better judge of a man than I am." He shoved a hand through his thick thatch of gray hair. "After you disappeared, I had my private investigator dig into Ryan Bratton's background a little deeper. I also had my team of accountants check into his corporate dealings. What I found scared the crud out of me. I didn't know if you'd left of your own volition, or if Bratton kidnapped you. I had no idea Bratton was stealing from the company. I thought he was a good match—a forward-thinking young man with a bright future ahead of him. Someone who could give you everything you deserve."

Phoebe snorted. "Well, I didn't deserve him." She touched her father's arm. "I always did what you and Mama wanted of me, but I never felt like I belonged in your world." She glanced around at her new friends. "Though I've only been here for a couple of days, I've never felt more at home and needed. I want to stay, preferably with your blessing. But, with or without it, I'm staying."

"You have it," her father said. "If this place makes you happy, let me help you get set up."

Phoebe shook her head. "Thanks, but I like making it on my own."

Her father nodded. "Fair enough. At least let me

find a vehicle for you to get around in. I hate to think of you stranded on the roadside."

"Being stranded on the roadside was where this adventure began." With a smile, Phoebe leaned into Nash's body. "I wouldn't have learned what a wonderful place Hellfire, Texas, was, or the generosity of its people if the car I was driving hadn't had a flat tire."

Nash's heart swelled in his chest. He couldn't believe she was staying. Having settled things with her father, she could have chosen to take the easy life and go back to Dallas. But she wanted to stay in Hellfire.

He looped an arm around her waist and held her against him, happy and optimistic about the future for the first time since he returned from the war. Nash realized what he'd been missing in his life. Not just a place to call home, but someone to come home to.

If he played his cards right, then Phoebe could be that someone. Now all he had to do was give her time to come around to his way of thinking. He'd show her what a loving, caring family could be, and let her decide for herself if this was what she wanted.

Within minutes, the crowd dispersed, trucks leaving one by one.

Audrey glanced around at the emptying parking lot. "I say we call it a night."

"I don't mind working through to regular closing time," Phoebe offered.

Nash stood by, hoping Audrey would give the girls the rest of the night off.

Audrey glanced at her watch. "Seems it's already closing time. And I, for one, need to be home in my bed." She winked at Jackson. "With the man I love."

Jackson took off his hat and shouted, "Yee-haw!" Then he scooped up Audrey, careful not to disturb her injured leg. "Charli, you can lock up."

Charli saluted. "Got it." She turned to the others standing around. "Let's call it a night."

"I'm headed back to Dallas," her father said. "Seems the only places to stay around here are booked through the weekend."

Phoebe grinned. "It's rodeo week."

"That's what they said." Mr. Sinclair hugged his daughter. "I know I don't show it enough, but I really do love you, Phoebe. You can always come home. Never forget that."

"I won't," she whispered.

Her father climbed into his SUV with the bodyguards and left.

"Now that you're no longer in danger, you could go back to your apartment over Lola's garage," Nash offered.

Phoebe took both of his hands. "What do you want me to do?"

"Uh-uh." He shook his head. "I want you to do what *you* want to do."

Taking his hand, she grinned. "Since my clothes are all at your place...I think it's best if I stay there tonight. If that's okay with you."

Relief washed over him. "Babe, it's more than okay. That goes right along with my plan."

"Oh?" She cocked her brows. "And what plan is that?"

"To win you over with my charm and good looks."

"Hmm. And if that doesn't work, you can always flash your badge." She rose on her toes and whispered in his ear, "I'm a sucker for a man in uniform."

"And I can't resist a runaway bride." He scooped her into his arms and carried her to his truck, settling her on the passenger seat. Before he closed the door, he leaned inside and kissed her long and hard, sweeping his tongue across hers in a promise of more to come.

"I never thought getting stranded on the roadside could be so good," she said, brushing a finger along his jaw.

"And I never thought coming home would ever feel right again." He held her close for a long time, inhaling the sweetness that surrounded his auburn-haired beauty. "I didn't know home was only missing you."

SEAL'S HONOR

TAKE NO PRISONERS SERIES BOOK #1

New York Times Bestselling Author
Elle James

TAKE NO PRISONERS
TUCK & DELANEY
BOOK 1

SEAL's
Honor

New York Times & USA Today Bestselling Author
ELLE JAMES

CHAPTER 1

REED TUCKER, TUCK to his buddies, tugged at the tie on his U.S. Navy service dress blue uniform, and his gut knotted as he entered the rehabilitation center of the National Naval Medical Center in Bethesda, Maryland.

He'd never run from anything, not a machine gun pinning his unit to a position, a fight where he was outnumbered, or an argument he truly believed in. But the sights, smells, and sounds inside the walls of the rehabilitation center made him want to get the hell out of the facility faster than a cat with its tail on fire.

But he couldn't leave. Not yet. This was graduation day for Reaper, aka Cory Nipton, his best friend and former teammate on SEAL Team 10. Reaper was being released from the rehabilitation center after enduring something even tougher than BUD/s training, the twenty-four week Basic Underwater Demolition/SEAL training designed to weed out the true SEALs from the wannabes.

But Reaper's release from rehab wasn't the only event that brought Tuck there that day. He was going to a wedding. His heart twisted, his palms grew clammy, and he clutched

the ring box in his left hand as regret warred with guilt, creating a vile taste in his mouth.

Reaper was marrying Delaney, the only woman Tuck had ever trusted with his heart. The only woman who'd forced him to get over his past and dare to dream of a future. She was the woman he could see himself spending the rest of his life with. And today she was promising to love, honor, and cherish his best friend—a better man than Tuck by far. A hero who'd lost his right arm because Tuck hadn't given him sufficient cover. Cory deserved all the happiness he could get after being medically discharged out of the only family he'd ever known. The Navy SEALs.

His hand on the door to the room where the wedding was to take place, Tuck squared his shoulders and stepped into his future.

Two months earlier

TUCK GLANCED TO his left and right. The members of Strike Force Dragon sat or stood, tense, holding onto whatever they could as the MH-60M Black Hawk dipped into the valley between two hilltops, less than a click away from the dark, quiet village. The only thing different about this mission was that, since the one before, he'd slept with the Pilot in Command of the helicopter.

Most men knew her as Razor, the call sign they used for the only female pilot flying infiltration and extraction missions for the 160th Special Operations Aviation Regiment (SOAR), Army Captain Delaney O'Connell.

Through his NVGs he picked up the bright green signature of a lookout on top of one of the buildings.

Within seconds, shots were fired at them, tracer rounds flaring in the dark. The helicopter remained just out of range of the man's rifle shots, but it wouldn't be long before a Taliban machine gunner with long-range capability was alerted with the potential of lobbing rocket-propelled grenades their way.

Wasting no time, the helicopter sank to a level just above the drop zone (DZ). While it hovered the men fast-roped down.

As soon as his boots hit the ground, Tuck brought up his M4A1 in the ready position and ran toward the sniper on the rooftop, zigzagging to avoid being locked in the enemy crosshairs.

Reaper, Big Bird, Gator, Fish, and Dustman spread out to the sides and followed.

When they were in range, Reaper took a knee and

employed his uncanny ability as a sharpshooter to knock off the sentry on the rooftop.

The team continued forward into the walled town, going from building to building, until they reached the one they were after. In the center of the compound, high walls surrounded one particular brick and mud structure.

Big Bird bent and cupped his hands.

Tuck planted his boot in the man's massive paws and, with Big Bird's help, launched himself to the top of the wall, dropping down on the other side in a crouch. Weapon pointing at the building, finger on the trigger, Tuck scanned the courtyard for potential threat. People moved past windows inside. So far, no one had stepped outside to check out the disturbance. Only a matter of time. "Clear," he said into his headset.

As Dustman topped the wall, a man emerged from the side of the structure and fired on them.

Without hesitation, Tuck fired off a silent round, downing the man with one bullet.

Dustman dropped to the ground beside him and gave him a thumbs up, taking the position by the wall so Tuck could move to the corner where the dead man lay.

As they'd discussed in the operations briefing, they only had three minutes to get into the compound, retrieve their target, and get out. Kill anyone in the way, but bring out the target alive.

Once four of the six-man team were inside the wall, they breached the doorway and entered, moving from room to room. If someone or something moved, they had only a millisecond to decide whether or not to shoot.

Tuck opened the first room. Inside, small green heat signatures glowed in his NVGs. Children sleeping on mats on the floor. He eased shut the door, jamming a wedge in the gap to keep them from getting out too soon.

He moved on to the next room. When he opened the door, a woman rose from a pallet, wearing a long black burka. When she lifted her hand like she held a gun, Tuck fired, taking her down before she could pull the trigger.

As he continued in the lead position down the narrow hallway, Tuck's adrenaline hammered blood through his veins and honed his senses. His wits in hyper-alert status, his finger rested a hair's breadth away from again pulling the trigger. This was the life he was made for. Defending his country, seeking out his enemies and destroying them with a swift, deadly strike. His job was risky, dangerous, and deadly.

A man emerged from a room down the hall.

Tuck's nerves spiked. He had only a fraction of a second to identify him.

Not his target.

He pulled the trigger and nailed him with another

silent round. The man slumped to the floor, his cry for help nothing more than a startled gasp.

The door he'd emerged from flew open and men bearing guns poured out.

Tuck spoke quietly into his headset. "Get down." He didn't bother to look back. His team would follow his orders without hesitation. He dropped with them, his M4A1 in front of him, and fired at the kneecaps of the men filling the hallway.

One by one, they went down, discharging their weapons, the bullets going wide and high.

In Pashto, the language spoken by most of the population of Afghanistan and Pakistan, Tuck told them to lay down their weapons.

When one of the injured enemies sat up and took aim, Tuck fired another round, putting him out of the game.

The injured enemy soldiers threw down their guns.

"Gator, clean up out here," Tuck whispered into his mic. "Reaper and Big Bird, you're with me."

In the lead, Tuck stepped around the fallen Taliban and entered the room in a low crouch, ducking to the right. Nothing moved. Another door led into yet another unknown space. Tuck dove into the room and rolled to the side, weapon up.

As he entered, a man with an AK47 fired off a burst of rounds that whizzed past Tuck's ears, missing him, but not by much. The man shouted for Tuck to drop his weapon.

Tuck fired at the shooter's chest. He fell to the ground, revealing the man he'd been protecting. Their target, the Taliban leader they'd been briefed on. He stood straight, a pistol aimed at Tuck.

Though he wanted to pull the trigger, Tuck couldn't shoot. His mission was to bring him out alive.

His hesitation cost him. A round, fired point-blank, hit him in the chest and flung him backward to land on his ass. If not for the armor plate protecting him, he'd be a dead man. He lay still for a moment, struggling to regulate his breathing.

Reaper used the stun gun, firing off a round that hit dead on and had the man flat on his back and twitching in seconds. "You okay?" He extended his hand to help Tuck to his feet.

"Yeah." Tuck motioned to Big Bird. "Take him."

The biggest, strongest man of the team, Big Bird lifted their target and flung him over his shoulder.

Still fighting to catch his breath, Tuck led the way back to the fence. Once outside the building, he scanned his surroundings and then checked back up at the top of the roof. No signs of enemy snipers. But that didn't mean they were in the clear. They still had to navigate their way out of town and get back to the helicopter.

Leading the way, with Gator and Fish guarding

the rear, Tuck hurried back along the narrow street to the outer walls of the village where the helicopter hovered nearby, waiting for their signal.

Tuck blinked the flashlight outfitted with a red lens at the hovering aircraft and it moved in, setting down for the briefest of moments, enough to get the six-man team inside. He reached over the back of the seat to the pilot and shouted, "Go!"

The Black Hawk lurched into the air, rising up and moving forward at the same time, hurrying to gain as much altitude as possible as they disappeared into the night sky, out of enemy sight and weapons range.

Not until they were well out of reach did Tuck release the breath he'd been holding and take stock of his team and their prisoner. All of them made it out alive and intact. That's the way he liked it. He'd been the only one who would have sustained injury if he hadn't been equipped with armor plating.

The co-pilot handed Tuck an aviation headset and he slipped it on.

"Nine minutes, twenty-five seconds." Gunnery Sergeant Sullivan's raspy voice sounded in Tuck's ear. "Better, but still not fast enough."

This had been a training mission, one they'd repeated five times in the past two weeks. Someone wanted them to get it right. The team was improving, but still needed to be quieter, faster, and more aware when the mission was real. The people they'd shot tonight had only been tagged with lasers. If this mission went live, the ammunition used against them would be live rounds.

Leaning back, Tuck held up nine fingers for his team to see and understand the repercussions of wearing out their welcome in a Taliban-held village.

The men nodded. Noise from the rotors precluded talking inside the chopper. When they got back to the base at Little Creek, Virginia, they'd debrief before being dismissed for the night and hitting the club.

They'd played the same scenario five times, improving with each iteration. All six members of the team were highly

skilled Navy SEALs. The cream of the crop, the most highly disciplined officers and enlisted men from the Navy.

Like Tuck, the team was tired of playing pretend. They wanted to get in and do the job. But, like most missions, they didn't know when they would go, who their target would be, or where they'd have to go to take him out. Only time and their commanding officers would tell. Only when they were about two hours out would they get their final orders and all the details.

In the meantime, they'd be off duty until the following morning's PT, unless orders came in that night. It happened. But if Tuck waited around his apartment for it to come about, he'd go stir-crazy.

Besides, he wanted to see O'Connell and pick up where they'd left off the night before.

BACK AT BASE, Delaney O'Connell climbed out of the pilot's seat and grabbed her flight bag. Adrenaline still thrumming through her veins, she knew going back to her apartment for the night wasn't an option.

Her co-pilot, Lt. Mark Doggett, aka K-9, fell in step beside her. "The team's headed to DD's Corral for a beer and some dancing. I know you don't usually like to hang out, but it's been a tough week. Wanna go?"

"Sure," she said, a little too quickly. Any other time, she'd have cut him off with a quick, but polite, *no*. But if she went back to her apartment alone, Tuck might show up and what good would that bring? Somehow, she'd fallen off the abstinence wagon with a vengeance and she was having a hard time getting back on.

"Great." K-9 cleared his throat. "Do you need a ride?" "No, thank you. I prefer to drive myself."

"Probably a good idea. These Navy guys work hard and play harder."

As well she knew. Tuck had played her in bed like a musician played an electric guitar, hitting every one of her chords like a master.

Her body quivered with remembered excitement, her core heating to combustible levels. Maybe going to the club was a bad idea. If Tuck was there...

She squared her shoulders. They didn't call her Razor for nothing. She would cut him off like she'd done so many others who'd tried getting too close. And soon. Walking away from a physical relationship was a hell of a lot easier than walking away from an emotionally involved one. Delaney refused to invest her emotions in another man with an addiction to adrenaline rushes. She'd been there once and would not go there again.

Before Tuck, she'd gone two years without a man in her life. Two years since Mad Max, Captain Chase Madden, bought it on a leadership interdiction mission in Pakistan. When a Special Forces soldier had been left behind, he'd gone back into hostile territory against his commanding officer's order. His helicopter had been shot down. Max had been injured, but was still alive until the Taliban found him and dragged him through the streets tied to the back of a truck. By the time they untied him, he'd bled out.

Delaney had been devastated. No one knew she and Mad Max had gotten engaged two weeks prior to his deployment. And no one would, if she could help it. Being a part of the 160th Special Operations Aviation Regiment was an honor she took very seriously.

She understood her position was precarious. On more than one occasion, her CO had told her she was on probation as the only female ever entrusted with the honor of flight leader in an all-male corps. The powers that be were watching her every move. One misstep and she would be out, and she'd worked too damned hard to get here. Three years of training, and working her way up the food chain, and a rock- hard body, at least where it counted, had gotten her noticed.

Fooling around with Tuck, one of the Navy SEALs assigned to this training mission, wouldn't go over well with her commander. But the strain of anticipation and the long bout of celibacy had taken their toll on Delaney. She'd needed a release. When Tuck and Reaper offered to help her change her flat tire, she never dreamed she'd end up in bed with one of them. But those damned SEALs with their massive biceps and quads...

Holy shit. What a mistake. And Tuck would probably think their liaison meant something.

Which it didn't.

She didn't need a man in her life. Not when her missions were as dangerous as they were. And a relationship with a SEAL was as dumb as it got. Her in the Army, him in the Navy. Both deployable at a moment's notice and most likely to opposite ends of the earth. Only Kismet was what brought them together at Little Creek, Virginia, to train for a possible mission. If they deployed together, their sleeping together would only complicate matters.

And she needed a clear head to complete the missions she would be responsible for flying.

Tonight, she'd tell Tuck not to expect anything. She wasn't into commitment or the long-term relationships.

ABOUT THE AUTHOR

ELLE JAMES also writing as MYLA JACKSON is a *New York Times* and *USA Today* Bestselling author of books including cowboys, intrigues and paranormal adventures that keep her readers on the edges of their seats. With over eighty works in a variety of sub-genres and lengths she has published with Harlequin, Samhain, Ellora's Cave, Kensington, Cleis Press, and Avon. When she's not at her computer, she's traveling, snow skiing, boating, or riding her ATV, dreaming up new stories. Learn more about Elle James at www.ellejames.com

Website | Facebook | Twitter | GoodReads | Newsletter | BookBub | Amazon

Or visit her alter ego Myla Jackson at mylajackson.com
Website | Facebook | Twitter | Newsletter

Follow Me!
www.ellejames.com
ellejames@ellejames.com